HE IS HERE

Jon Riols

ISBN: 978-0-9575068-0-0

'In memory of all the men and women who have suffered or not, trying to make this world a better place for all.'

CHAPTER I

"I am Alive," I said out loud as if words were coming from all my being, "Thank You."

After breakfast, I grabbed my bag and called doggy. We left the house for the hills.

As we passed Suzie's house, she was just at her front door.

"Hey, hello young man," she said.

"Oh! Hi, Suzie, you're up early?" I replied.

"Yeah, last night I got so emotional after I met a very beautiful person at the stadium and, oh, yes, how? What? Yes, I do, Oh! I am in Love," she added.

"Wow, what news! I am so glad for you."

"Yeah, but I can't sleep, I'm so excited, over the moon."

"Ahahaha, fabulous, oh, I'm so pleased."

"Hey! What are you up to? I'm off to the hills with Purl. She's in a bit of a cranky mood this morning. She can smell something is in the air. And she needs to dry out. Want a lift?" she asked.

"Eh? Yep! Sounds great! I hope you don't mind but I won't

be joining you for the walk. I've got things to do," I replied.
"Oh! Yeah? Like what?"
"Well, today is that one day in the year when I carve
wooden spoons."
"You?…What? WHAT? OH! I'm so sorry. I forgot, I
should have said first. Oh! I'm so sorry. HAPPY
BIRTHDAY. Oh wow, come on! Jump in the car. And you,
Lou, how are you? You're so beautiful. Kiss, kiss, kiss, kiss.
Oh, I love you.
Come on now all of you, in the car!" she instructed.

"Oh, I could not sleep, tossing and turning in bed, laughing!
Smiling! Crying! Talking! Oh, P.A.L.P.I.T.A.T.I.N.G! So, I
got up and did the ironing, cleaning up, washed Purl… I
mean everything to distract me!" she said as soon as we sat
down.
"Yeah?"
"Oh! Am so excited, we are meeting for dinner at 'Take me
Out' around the corner. Oh! Dear! WHAT AM I GOING
TO WEAR?" she never stopped.
"Euuuhhh."
"Shall I invite him back home? Tell me what you think,
please. And what am I going to wear?"
"Maybe you should go to Local Market"
"Oh! I don't know, I should call Tina, I'm sure she can
help," she concluded.

We were approaching the car park as the sun was already
warming this fresh September morning.
"Hey, want to come for some tea and cakes at the farm?
Maybe we'll be lucky, some might be left," she asked.
"Suzie, I told you, I have something to do! So, not now,
let's catch up later."
"Oh! I'm sorry to be such a pain."
"You are not a pain" I reassured her.
"Well, you know, I'm so excited but tired and all those

emotions, oh! I can't stop."
"OK! Now, see you later Suzie. Come on Lou. Hey! Look!
Purl has already started. Come on! Go!"
"OK! OK! See you soon. I mean you know I'm just such
in…" she gushed.

I did not hear what she said when I left. I walked ten
minutes. It was such a pleasant morning. A bunch of clouds
were pushing slowly through the valley bellow. The view
was impressive from this dry highway. Some clouds were
attached to long darker tubes that in some way were
connected to the ground, gigantic mushrooms causing
shaded areas in this sunny land.
'How many years have I walked this way?' I thought, '29
years today,' I remembered, '29.' Yes I was 9, the first time I
came here with my dad. Well, 29 including the 4 years I
travelled and actually did not come here to make spoons. I
remembered I followed him up the first hill, being steep, it
did not attract many people, and then we walked along the
same pathway that I used to find long and strenuous, at first
but always so quiet. Finally we turned left.

Here we are. The Old Oak has been here for years. For
more than 29 years I have been coming here for sure, and I
remembered it as being already very impressive. The big
stone underneath it was still there and I sat on it as it has
always been.
Lou was doing his own businesses, sniffing hedges and
woods for lost balls or food. He never goes too far from
me so that he can keep an eye on me. As it was of no
concern, I started on my spoons.

I was finishing my fifth spoon when I heard Suzie calling
Purl to come to her. I packed my tool and spoons. Lou,
who was chewing on wood near the stone, got up and we
joined them.

I usually keep the first spoon for myself. I gave one to Suzie that I engraved with her name.

"What do you want to give me a spoon for? It's not Christmas!" she said.

"To thank you for driving and because I want to! Well I'd like to! You were here with me this morning and all in love. It would make me very happy," I added.

"Don't be silly. It's my pleasure. I need someone to talk to, I am so exhausted now. I'm going to bed as soon as I'm back; I need to stay awake 'til then. I accept your spoon, and it makes me very happy."

"If you use it, please rub cooking oil on it once in a while to prevent the wood from breaking, alright?" I warned her.

"OK, let's go!" she ordered.

Every Saturday, and today was no exception, I would work at the animal centre. There were so many of us working there that each person only had to give a few hours and we were all so enthusiastic about it that no one wanted to leave and no one at the moment was signed off. It was always appreciated when one or more were away, as the waiting list was big and many were happy to come only occasionally. For me, it was my last Saturday there, at least for the time being. For how long? I wasn't sure.

I started to work there when I was 16, Saturday morning from 10am to 12 noon, to clean the boxes. It was after a car hit our doggy, Zork. As they have an animal repair centre we came there. And I fell in love with the place and its achievements. Slowly, I was introduced to all the facets of the enterprise.

I didn't work much that day; they were waiting for me with a surprise buffet at the main reception. They had asked some part-timers if they would be happy to cover.

There were a variety of teas, herbal ones, fruits and fruit juices, toast and cakes.

Henrietta was there as she is every Saturday, only she wasn't working in her coordinator's office. She gave me my 'leaving book', as she loves to call them.

She is amazing. She loves following people and marking the big events in their lives. Not only was she doing it for members of her family and friends, but also acquaintances. Sometimes strangers asked after her: "That's her!"

She loved it so much that she started offering to do it for companies and social offices. It was simple; she required every business to have boxes individually named with every employee's name. Everyone in the company was encouraged to fill any boxes, whenever required, with souvenirs, memos, pictures, letters, dry flowers… anything that could be added to the leaving book of the person named on the box. When a person was to leave, their box was simply sent to Henrietta's centre where they produced that person's leaving book. Sometimes it was just a few pages; other times reams.

In my case, it was a good volume filled with memories, my second leaving book from this animal centre.

She created this job in her early youth out of her own passion and it has spread very quickly. It was brilliant and many towns and cities around the word started to do the same. Ah! Internet! What a great way to spread ideas, projects and start building communities of people into the same things.

'The Henrietta's' is her company name. She offers a great service and we love her.

My book was signed with little memos on the front and back by present colleagues. Even Henrietta had signed after a 'Well-done' drawing she had made encrusting animal heads in every letters. Again, there was a very small 'sorry' written before her signature. Sorry for what? I guessed again, probably because I was leaving.

I hugged everyone goodbye and promise I will return as soon as possible.

Back home, I only took Lou in front of the house, on the crescent. I was not hungry after the party so I just hung around Lou waiting for him to do his business. He was funny, making circles for ages before dropping his stuff. I went to pick it up when I noticed next to it a dirty piece of glass under some leaves. When I picked it up, it was actually a little purple square stone with a black broken necklace attached to it. It must have fallen from someone's neck a few days ago. I put it in my pocket and went home for a relaxing afternoon before the party.

The party was in a wood, not too far from home. I haven't been to this kind of party for some time now, if I think about it. But it was special tonight, it was 'The Stallions', a musician nomad tribe that I met when I was travelling. Angelina will be there, Angelina, my ex and Dick.

I decided to take the train to the station nearest to the woodland and then walk to the party from there.
I was sat at the end of the compartment on the right side when a young woman sat opposite, on the left. She was beautiful, pink hair, tight denim trousers and a short white t-shirt under some braces attached to the trousers. She kept looking at me, smiling, wanting to say something, showing me the books she was reading, trying to catch my attention. I could not keep my eyes away from her for too long but kept silent. Something in me was saying, 'you'll meet her again and this time it will be The Time.' I wasn't sure but that feeling was so strong, it paralyzed my lips…we never exchanged any words. You know, it even looked like she never got off at the station she was meant to but left the train when I left, only to go to the other side of the platform.

"Hey SEXY, you're here...Yeahhhh come here!"
Here she was, Angelina, as wild as ever, on her knees around a fire, suntanned, wearing a black bra and a black ¾ length very low rise type trousers made of loose fabric. Her hair had grown long now but she had shaved a side off around her right ear to reveal the leopard print tattoo that started on top of that ear and turned around the head down the right side of the neck. It was like it was infused with her skin. She was still wearing her left nostril-piercing ring.

"So you got my message? I didn't get any reply, so I wasn't sure you would come. You are still crap at telepathy as I can see," she grinned.
"So why don't you phone me if you expect a reply?" I smiled.
"You haven't changed, gorgeous as ever!"

We hugged for few minutes.

"So, Angie, how is it going? It's been a while" I asked.
"First, Happy Birthday mister. I hope you enjoy my present. Soon you should go near the dance floor and warm up, hehehehe" she laughed, "I am so happy you came. We haven't been around here for ages, if ever, it seems."

Angelina was one of those disc jockeys who never recorded any of her mixes. She had fans, followers, admirers all around the globe, only by word of mouth. She was very special indeed.
For a start she never stepped foot in cities or towns, rather farms to villages. And she was friends with 'The men of the woods.'
She was a Vegan, she belongs to the Vegetarian Police and to the Peacefullers, and of course, she was an expert in mechanics, technology and computers.

"I am very glad to see you indeed. How's Dick?"

"Dick is around somewhere. He's alright. We are still together…15 years now, eh? I'm more committed as the years pass by. I still have few favorites in the woods but nothing serious, only pleasure.

I'll make some tea, a special blend for your enjoyment tonight. It should be perfect timing. You still trust me, don't you?"
"Sure Angie, please do, thank you, and not too strong. I'm not so used to it nowadays."
"Do you know I am still using your spoon? The one you made for me. I love it. It travels everywhere with me."

I loved that, one of my spoons on the other side of the globe, the idea that something I have made was useful to someone somewhere.

Angelina and I met on a dance floor. I was dancing next to her and we hadn't noticed each other until someone pointed at both of us with a big smiling face. She was wearing a sleeveless black mini dress and was barefoot. She had the tattoo on her right side of the head and a ring in the left nostril. I was wearing black trousers, bare top with a tiger tattoo on my left shoulder and a ring on my right nostril. We hugged and stayed together for 2 years, the 2 last years of my travelling years.

One night, she caught Dick and I playing behind a bush at a party. "Can I join?" she asked, rubbing herself in between us.
And she was still with him now. Well, I could understand. We had too many differences to stay together and I wanted a more sedentary life. She couldn't and surely still can't understand why I need to structure my days. We always argued about this.
"I don't have a routine in my life" she used to say, "I am free, to wake up when I want, to sleep when I want, to

eat/drink when I want, I don't have a routine!"
"Yes you do have routines," I used to reply, "and each time you wake up, what do you do? Do you make yourself the same tea everyday?"
She was so stubborn that she was actually trying her best to change drinks, anything that would look like she didn't have a routine. I mean maybe it was true. Something for sure is that she was very self-disciplined.

"Hey, by the way, I need to tell you that something has changed. I now drink a glass of water every morning when I wake up. Don't get too excited! That is the only roooooutine I have," she said suddenly, as if reading my thoughts.

"Are you going to Muktor's winter festival?" She asked.
"Yes, it's in my plan. This year I feel like doing it again. I haven't been since when we were there together and I'll soon be 40. You never know, one day, I might meet someone who doesn't like those kinds of things. So yes. I'm going."
"Great, we'll be there too. We are staying for the full two months of the festival. I have a lot of things with me to make a stall, from the travels and from 'The men of the woods'. You know how people love what those men make and there are so few of us in contact with them. I take the stuff out one by one and I love choosing who will have what. You can't find those things on those silly online things" she added.

We chatted for some time, enjoying this hot cup of tea before Dick arrived. He was such a strong man. I stayed a bit more and then left them together and went for a walk around the party, to see what the artists had drawn and the general circus that followed.

I was on my way to the dance floor when I heard the sound

of a tiger-like roar, reaching a crescendo, filling the woods. Everyone was silent…Angelina was at the decks!

I started to run toward the dance floor, I didn't want to miss a bit of my birthday present. The roar was transforming itself into 'droplets' that seemed to fall on the ground making the start of the beat. I positioned myself in the centre of the dance floor knowing that she would use all the speakers together, and in turn, to maximize the effect. And I was not wrong. It was Sensational!

CHAPTER II

I came back to bed, sat comfortably, looking at The Candle's flame, hands resting on my lap, palms down then closed my eyes.

"I am starting Hatsu Rei now," I said focusing my attention on my tandem point.

This morning it was particularly difficult for me to completely focus. I kept thinking of what was to come; soon Tristan will knock at the door.

Before taking Lou out in the crescent, I decided to prepare some pancake batter that I would cook for breakfast. I wasn't sure what form of diet Tristan was following, so I added 120g of flour with 275ml of hemp milk and a pinch of salt in a mixer. I always go for a vegan base meal when I don't know my guest. At least I am pretty sure that vegans, ovo–lacto, ovo- or lacto-vegetarians, flexitarians and non-vegetarians alike will be happy with it. If any of my guests eat animal flesh or are vegetarian, then I can add a flesh substitute to their plate.

Tristan rang the doorbell at 8am. He was an average size man, with blond short hair. He carried a big suitcase on wheels and a man bag over his shoulder.

"Good morning. You must be Tristan," I said smiling at the door. "Welcome to Brighton. Please do come in."
Tristan smiled in return: "You must be JR" and came in. "I have to be honest with you, I am feeling a bit lost right now" he said when we entered the kitchen-dining room.
"I am going to help you the best I can" I told him. "First I am going to show you your room, in case you want to freshen up a bit, and then we will go outside to get some food for Breakfast. I have not planned anything else for you for the rest of the day as I expect you may want to rest after all the events you have been through. And we'll have a lot to discuss. Please don't hesitate to ask for anything, I will do my best to answer you to the best of my knowledge. If you want to come with me, at 10am, I am going to do a bit of gardening but it is up to you."
"I think I'll stay in. We'll see. I'll be down in 15 minutes for breakfast, OK?" he asked.
"Sounds good but please don't hurry. We have time," I replied.

Tristan came down as he said.
"OK, I'm ready. How much do you think I need?" he asked.
"How much what?"
"Money. Do I need to change it? I don't even know what money you use here nowadays…sorry," he said.
"No, you don't need money. We are not going to play. We are just going to pop outside to pick up some apples, I have everything else we need I think. What's your diet?" I asked him.
"What do you mean?"
"Are you Vegan or Gluten-free or…?" I clarified.

"Oh no, I eat everything. I'm lucky because I have no food intolerances. What about you?"

"Let's say I'm more Vegan but Vegetarian socially. I mean when I'm alone I don't eat dairy products nor eggs, I do like honey though and when I am out, with friends, family or events, I accept vegetarian food," I replied.

"Why?"

"The majority of people today are ovo-lacto vegetarian. Therefore at most parties, and other social events, vegetarian food is offered, sometimes with a vegan option but usually, for example, the cakes are vegetarian," I explained.

"Oh, I see. Well where I come from, the majority of people eat fish, meat, eggs and dairy. To be honest we don't even offer many options in our social units."

"What do you mean, 'we don't offer many options?'" I asked.

"Well, when the island closed its frontiers just before the turn of the millennium. No one could come in or out until now. Yes! Pretty much one hundred years later! Well Our King and his government installed a law forbidding any social units, hospitals, jails, schools, and pensioners' houses to offer alternative diets. So, if you are vegan or vegetarian, you have to not eat the meat in your plate. It is so difficult for them. The meat juice is always everywhere. You can imagine all the deficiencies those people have unless they have someone from the outside providing them with food supplements. The only people exempted from such a regime are those who can prove, medically certified by government doctors, an allergy to a certain food," Tristan explained.

"Sounds impossible. Honestly, I can't even visualize a society that would do such a thing. Sorry, I didn't mean…I am here to show you our way not to judge. I am sorry," I apologized.

"Oh please, don't be sorry. On the contrary, please tell me

what you think about where I grew up and lived…. I am sure it will help me to understand this world even more."
"OK, I will then. Shall we go?" I asked.

"I prepared some pancake batter earlier on, what filling would you like Tristan? We have apples, figs, tomatoes, peppers and eggs at the communal garden in the crescent. This is where I go at 10 to help gardening. Most inhabitants around the crescent help whenever they like or can. It functions very well. A few are very engaged in it and they stay all day working. I come every Monday and Thursday mornings for 2 hours usually. Please take what you would like for breakfast. I have prepared enough for 2 pancakes each and 1 more but I can easily do even more if you want. I also have some strawberries and lettuce growing in my little indoor garden."
"Do you have honey?" asked Tristan.
"Yes I have some local honey made by a friend from the animal centre where I worked," I replied.
"Great, so it's free and I can take all that I want?" he asked.
"Yes it is free indeed but I would advise you to take just what you need. You will understand why later on," I advised him.
"OK, I'll have one with tomato, pepper and an egg to start with and one with honey and shredded apple. Can I have some fig and strawberry juice? You have a juicer?" he asked.
"Yes…that all sounds good. I'll have the same and you should try the blackberry jam and the dandelion jam I made this summer," I replied.
"Dandelion jam? Sounds yummy. I didn't know you could make jam from Dandelions."
"It's a family recipe from my great-grandmother on my father's side. We only use the yellow bits of the flowers. It's pretty simple really," I explained.

Back home, we went to the kitchen and started preparing

breakfast while chatting. He made the juice whilst I got the pancakes ready. I also brought the jams and some bread I had left over from the weekend, to the table.

"So Tristan, tell me, did you have a good journey getting here?" I asked.

"Yes but it was tiring to travel after all that happened recently on the island. I am a little scared too, to be honest. I didn't see much during the night travel but everything seemed peaceful. I took the plane last night from the newly opened airport, the only one re-opened to the world so far and landed at Gatwick this morning where a driver from the agency waited for me to bring me to your place. Everything looked normal. I mean pretty much as it is in the Island. I particularly find it fabulous to see all those fruit trees growing everywhere and I can see your technology has evolved…those cars and trucks look absolutely amazing. And I want to try those flying cars I saw on my way here. What surprised me though, was that I didn't get any I.D. check…nothing! I guessed it was due to where I come from and who I am," he explained.

"I.D. check? You are funny. We are not in the History era any more, we're in Post-History don't you know?" I laughed.

"Post-History? What are you talking about? The only thing we were told back home was that outside the Island; it was chaos, hell really…a place not to go!!! And now that our government and king have collapsed I am sent to see how it has all evolved, make a general statement that will be read to all inhabitants of the island to see if they want to join your world or not. We are a democratic institution now. Anyone from villages to big cities has to vote for anyone he or she likes for president. Each community keeps the three with the most votes. Then we pass to the departmental vote, then to the regional and finally to the national. The losers of each round can enter to be local town, departmental or regional mayor and deputies…a bit like we used to do to elect the island beauty queen. Of course the core government, the unseen, is staying. Me, I like it, I have money and I belong to those who stay rich. And I, honestly, don't understand why they sent me to you, and not to somebody from the government in London."

"The international agency that deals with your kind of request has selected me at random, as they mostly do in this kind of instance. To be on their list, of course, requires a Major in Post-History which I have, a few years travelling the world, which I did, knowing several languages and other little details which made me compatible. And I loved the idea. I was very happy when my name came up and I hope you will go back happy, happy to have met me and learnt all that you wanted. But I am sorry, I don't know much about History, other that what my granddad told me before he passed away. I never studied it at school. I didn't want to. I remember thinking that knowing History will not help me in my Life. Although I love those historic monuments and arts that have survived time, I don't like horror movies and it all seemed to me like a big horror movie that lasted for millennia. On Wednesday, we are going to London where we will visit Michael, he is a History teacher. I'm more interested, in fact very interested in what we call Post-History, everything that has happened since the Ivolution."

"The Ivolution?" Tristan asked.

"Before I was born, when my dad was a young man, something big happened on Earth" I replied, "we all call it The Ivolution. We chose the 21st of December as the celebration date because it is on that day that the first land started Post-History and inspired the rest of the world which very quickly followed. Of course, not all the world followed, such as your island, but also some underground cities locked themselves for few years. However, they missed the sunlight so much that they reopened very fast. Some territories on the East were encircled with walls to protect the reign of their form of society. We didn't really know what was going on there until they opened two decades ago. It was a major event for the world and to see the primal conditions they lived in. Many had returned to a savage way of living, half human-half beast. It is now taking years to humanize them back, but so far we are all happy with the results. It was and still is, of course, up to each and every one of them to decide how he or she wants to live. We are open. Even those who decided to live in their jungle are allowed to use our social services but they can't harm us."

"So I guess we, on our Island, are the last on earth who are still independent now, aren't we?" Tristan remarked.

"Yes, your Island is the last of the territories that refused the Ivolution. Now, I hope the time we will spend together will inspire you and encourage you to help your Island completely open its frontiers to the rest of the world. For now, you are the only one who has visited us as far as I know and still, none of us are allowed to visit your land. It is also said that a Queen with her subjects left for the sky and is building her own kingdom somewhere in space in a spacecraft. It might be a conspiracy, but if they did come back, the world army would be there to greet them."

"So you do have an army?"

"Yes we have a world army. Everyone can join in and train for any position they like but they all have a normal life, doing other jobs, many are full time Peacefullers. They have a special blue ring tattooed on their right ring finger. We have rarely need of an army now but it exists as a measure of security in case of an invasion of some kind, from space or underground or from your island. Each member will be called if any of those things happen and the weapon centers will open. Many of them play for their local paintball sport team," I explained.

"What about local armies? I mean national armies?"

"Well, since the Ivolution, there are no nations, so there is no need for national armies. All frontiers opened to create one world."

"Impossible!" Tristan exclaimed.

"You are funny. For us it is impossible to conceive that land could be separated into parts where inhabitants would be so proud of belonging to their part that they would even fight for it or expand it. No, we belong to one world, a big giant bubble," I told him.

"OK, so how does it work?" he asked.

"What do you mean, 'how does it work?'"

"I mean, OK, the Ivolution happened in 21st December of what year?" he added.

"Year 0 of course," I replied.

"No, it must have been 20-something, like 2005, 2012 or 2015, or later?" he continued.

"I'm sorry; I told you I don't know much of History. It happened on 21st of December and from the 1st of January that followed it was year 0. We have World Holidays from the 21st to the 1st every year for everyone. People can drive and travel by their own means during that time but no one is working on trains, buses, ferries, planes, or taxis. There are many pagans or religious parties meanwhile, especially on the 25th of December and the 31st of December. The only ones who work during that time are cleaners, firemen, ambulancemen, repairers, nurses, Peacefullers, forces, Vegetarian or Vegan Police officers, and the support staff needed to stay organized. They are either called or stay permanently on site, it is up to them."

"Hmm. I am not sure we will agree to that. We will certainly not agree to a world government," Tristan pointed.

"A world government? We don't have such a centralized thing. It sounds like an idea from History and I am not surprised that you are bringing it up," I laughed.

"So, how does it work?" asked Tristan. "How can you be without government? Has the world turn communist? From what I saw it cannot be anarchy."

"Commu… what? Now you are once again speaking from the History side. I remember my granddad talking about different forms of control that existed in those times but there is nothing like that anymore. When the land of the East opened, we learned that they decided to live in what was called anarchy, after they savagely killed their dictators and rich followers. And it was painful to see the results. Everything was devastated. Years, centuries, millennia of arts, architectures had vanished. It was very sad indeed, and painful, to see the lack of respect they had for their ancestors who had built for them a comfortable world. No! Everyone governs here, everyone on earth. Computers and technology allowed the Ivolution to happen. So, thank history for that. Like my granddad used to say 'it wasn't all bad'. Well, we all participate in a world survey on how we wish the world to be. The Computer is impartial to calculating the results of the survey but creates new questions on some issues that in turn appear on our screens for voting. The majority wins. There is no propaganda to influence votes. Everyone answers with an honest heart, knowing that we all want The Best for everyone and that now that everyone is living happily, I assure you everyone wants to maintain this Life. For example, if I think that we should install a new course in fashion schools, for example the option to learn latex garment making, then I type my question in the appropriate site and that question will be viewed in the 'ideas for a better world' pages under 'fashion'. When a question gets a certain number of answers or points, it moves to the 'general development voting' pages, also under the 'fashion' section, where most of us if not all of us, at least of the civilized world, vote. It works very well."

"So you have a un-civilized world?" Tristan asked.

"Well, people, communities who want to live self-sufficiently or the way their ancestors lived, in tepees, in trees… in abandoned farms. They are civilized but don't participate in our everyday life as such. They live independently. We mostly see them in the human repair centers, or schools where they need us," I explained.

"Are you talking about the hospital when you refer to repair centre?"

"Hospital? I don't know what hospital means. I never heard that name before. I am talking about the places where humans get repaired. When we fall down and break something for example or if we have an accident," I explained again.

"Where I come from, it's called a hospital. That is where people get treatment for their diseases and also to be 'repaired' as you are saying."

"It's pretty much the same here but we don't have many diseases any more. I mean nothing to worry about or lethal like my great-granddad had, although some people are unconscious and over-use some products. Most things are OK, not lethal, when taken in moderation. They teach us at school to use a variety of colors, shapes, breeds, groups and combinations. The cures came with the Ivolution, either because the laboratories were now focusing on cures rather than treatments or because some cures had been hidden, it is said, for business reasons. This I don't really understand. Let's not talk about all the plants that we discovered in the tropical forests and around the globe, that benefit humankind, now that researchers are looking everywhere and not limited as they were before. Although many food and lifestyle-associated diseases have vanished, we use herbs for example for colds and flu. One of the most important achievements we obtained was to totally annihilate that terrible disease they suffered and died from, back before the Ivolution called 'stress'. Many common ailments disappeared when we all became vegetarian. We are taught at school about basic indoor and outdoor gardening, herbal remedies and diet. So my generation at least, I was born in year 2, and all generations since then, as well as a few people born before me, know what to do. I think it's great. I loved the herbal classes. My teachers were great. My granddad used to say that in his time they had to vaccinate all newborn to prevent them from diseases that existed back then. He said some called it 'the mark of the beast'. All people had this mark caused by one vaccine. Many diseases were created in laboratories, he used to add, and it was like a response to their increasingly polluted world. Anyway, it will soon be 10am and I would love to go and work at the garden for a couple of hours if you don't mind. We will be travelling from Wednesday and therefore I want to say goodbye to my colleagues and neighbors there. Do you want to come?" I asked, while I was finishing the washing up from breakfast.

"No if you don't mind I am going to stay here, maybe I'll stay near the fireplace or I'll go up in my room. I don't know yet. I am feeling very lost. I need to think," replied Tristan.

"You might need to rest more than you think for now. I'll see you later, just before lunch. We'll decide then what you want to do."

"OK, thank you for everything but one more thing…what is the date today then?"

"Monday the 1st of October."

"What year please?"

"40."

"Thank You. I have to say I am feeling very lost and a lot of questions are spinning in my mind."

"Would you like me to stay?"

"Thank you for your offer, but please don't, I need to be alone for a while. It's just you've said so much already and there are many things that I don't understand or know what you are talking about. For now, I need to calm my head, write some notes and some questions to ask you. See you later!"

"OK, and please don't hesitate to help yourself with

whatever you need. You will find some relaxant in that box near the fireplace," I told him.

When I returned, after midday, Tristan was in his room. He had left a note on the dining table: 'Sorry, I don't feel very well. I am going to rest for a while. Don't worry about me for lunch. If I need anything I will ask. Please leave me a note if you are going out so that I know what is happening. Thank You. Sincerely, Tristan'.

CHAPTER III

It was only towards the end of the afternoon when Tristan came down to the kitchen-dinning room. His eyes were puffy from just awakening; he had not bothered brushing his hair.

"Good morning!" I said with a big smile "come and sit down near the fireplace. Would you like some tea? Or coffee? Or a cold drink? Anything to eat?"

"A cup of tea would be great. Thank you, with milk and 2 sugars."

I started to prepare the teas and I opted for a chamomile tea with honey.

"You have a lovely home," said Tristan, "I love the space…and it's on two floors! I had a look at your garden outside and indoors. You have some strange plants growing. I mean forbidden ones. It must cost a lot of money. Are you renting it or do you own it?" Tristan asked. "I'm glad you like my space. Well, in your terms, let's say I own it but rent it at the same time. Forbidden plants?"

"Yes," said Tristan, "I mean you have to be careful, with those illegal plants. I noticed that you also use them. I looked in the box you told me about."

"And? Why should I be careful?" I smiled.

"Well surely they are still illegal, aren't they? I mean marijuana and stuff?"

"Illegal! Are you joking? How can a plant, any plant in fact be illegal? They are here. It is not like something a human has created which would be dangerous or hazardous, is it? It is nature. It is there, and for all of us to love, to understand and to use! Are plants forbidden in your Island?" I asked.

"Yes marijuana is illegal in our Island as is chamomile and parsley. There were a few others but at soon as we became a democracy, we tolerated them," he explained.

"And who decides such absurdities?" I was shocked.

"Well, our government of course. And it is not absurd! They have their experts who say that those plants are dangerous and we believe them. Why would they lie to us?"

"I don't know, but it is absurd to me, especially marijuana that we use so much today. I mean, look at my shirt, it is hemp, marijuana, this is hemp. The cars outside, they run on hemp oil, the paper that we use for printing is hemp, the new houses are built with hemp. We use it in medicine; we use it to get stoned, some people to get creative. How on earth, can it be banned? It is absolutely ridiculous. And it saved the planet!"

"What do you mean? It saved the planet?" Tristan asked.

"Hemp saved the planet. After the Ivolution, we used hemp in almost everything like I just told you. It seems History had left us with a sad planet, very disturbed by the pollution the humans caused back then and all they did to the animals. But using hemp has very quickly reversed earth to the glorious and beautiful planet it is today."

"Again, it does sound unbelievable. I am not sure my government and its nation will allow that."

"If you are interested, you can find plenty of books on the uses and benefits of marijuana. I am sure you could take some of them back to show your government's experts the truth about it."

"OK, I'll think about it. Of course it will be on my report."

"If it must be. I don't really see why this is such an issue, maybe because it will show your nation, as you are calling it, that they can't trust their government nor experts? Will I be able to look at the end report? Out of curiosity that is," I asked.

"Yes, I will let you read it. You are welcome to write something as well if you think it can help us to make the final decision, but I don't want to elaborate on the last issue right now. We have a lot more to discuss. I want you to clarify some points I learned this morning. Please, will you wait while I go up and fetch my notes? Thank you."

"No worries," I concluded.

When Tristan returned, he was holding a notepad made of very lustrous white paper sheets. A few notes were on the first page, it rather seemed like a collection of words listed one after another.

"Your paper doesn't look like hemp paper" I joked. Tristan nodded quickly at me with an irritated look and wrote on the corner of the page and then encircled 'Marijuana is legal. It saved the planet'.

"OK, let's start!" he said.

CHAPTER IV

"We are Monday the 1st of October 40, is that correct?"
Tristan asked.

"Yes."

"And you are born in year 2, is that correct?"

"Yes."

"So you are 38?"

"Yes."

"Like me. OK, do you, by any chance, know your dad's birthday?"

"Well, sure, my dad is 58 years old. He was 20 when I was born. The Ivolution happened just when he finished the second school at 18," I replied.

"I mean do you know his date of birth?"

"No, I don't. It was before Post-History and when we changed calendar to year 0, the people alive decided to remember only their age from that date. Some even changed their names. They erased all the birthday year records as to start a fresh life. Only those born from the 1st of January 0 had their birthday year recorded. Do you know there are some people who went further and forgot their ages? I heard that some of them believe that now we will all be eternal, so what is the point of knowing one's age?"

"Thank you. Let me tell you, we are in 2052 of my calendar," Tristan told me.

"Well, I am happy you know, but isn't it a bit useless for me to know that information?" I laughed.

"Oh! OK, now, I am intrigued by your name, JR, if we can call it a name" Tristan smiled.

"Yes it is my name, and I don't have any other name officially. It comes from my granddad who in the time of History was given the nick name JR, standing for Just Real. He always used to say 'Just be Real' to his fellows during those dark human times, and they used to warn each other by saying 'Just Real is here' and that became 'JR is here'. He was a carpenter. I mean, you know, they always give themselves nicknames in those builder jobs. And my dad was called JR junior until my granddad died few years ago when he became JR. My granddad fell from a tree, collecting apples. It was the last time he pretended to be a monkey! My dad called me JR, and registered it as my official name."

"Can it be official? These are initials only," said Tristan, looking surprised.

"Not here. If you want to call your son 'A', here you are allowed, as much as if you want to call him 'Born on a warm Friday evening'. It is the parents' choice. Of course most people still give their children two or three names and most have kept their family name. The child, once an adult, may decide to add a new name, a kind of official nickname."

Tristan was now writing notes, pretty much everything I said. I waited until he finished before offering him more to drink or to eat.

"Not yet" he replied. "I'd like to go on a bit more right now

before dinner if that's OK with you?" he asked.
"Sure."

"This morning, before we went out, I asked you if I needed money and you replied something like 'we are not going to play.' What did you mean?"

"In our world, Post-History, we don't use money other than in a few games, a few card games. But more and more people are loosing interest in them, they prefer bingo or lotto. It's more fun. At least they feel they win something," I explained.
"So what do you use as exchange value?" he asked.
"Pardon?"
"What do you give when you want something? If you want to buy some bread, how do you pay? When you take the train? Or the plane?"
"Nothing."
"What? Nothing?"
"Everything is free as is everyone here," I told him.
"What? Nothing? That's impossible!"
"I don't see why it should be impossible. It works very well."
"But surely…"
"It works very well and everyone works, if that is what you want to know," I added, trying to reassure him.
"But how can it be?"
"People are not lazy. Some people give themselves totally to one job and others do many things, like me, and some study. It all works perfectly. Everyone does what he or she loves."
"Well, that is crazy. I can't think of how it can work properly. It is all so very different to what I expected."
"Michael, in London, will tell you more about how it happened. All I know is that we get very bored, us humans, if we don't do something. Therefore everyone does what he

31

or she likes and it is perfect. For example, my work schedule at the moment is usually 4 hours gardening at the local community garden per week, that I spilt in two mornings, Mondays and Thursdays and 2 hours at the animal centre on a Saturday morning. On Monday and Friday mornings I study Parapsychology at the moment. I am fascinated. On Wednesdays, all day, I work outside the city, cultivating land and collecting surplus of fruits for the local markets and for shipping. Every afternoon, I write, as my main ambition is to be an author. I write books and articles for the local Sunday newspaper. I usually keep my Sunday free."

"That sounds like fun. I still don't understand how it can truly work so well but I am sure after a few weeks, I will become more open to the idea. I mean you are telling me, I can go into a shop, like one of the shops I saw on my way here, and take whatever I want? Are you telling me, if I see a house I like I can take it and live in it? You're telling me everything is free!" he pointed.

"Yes, indeed, everything is free and priceless. Of course you can take all that you want, but do you need it all? Knowing tomorrow you can also have it for free and the day after and the day after, forever? Don't you think you just finish by taking what you just need? You can take any house you like as long as it is not occupied. You can find a repertoire of the unoccupied properties at local centers. Every adult is allocated at least a two bedroom flat with an indoor garden. It is up to each one to decide if he or she prefers an outdoor garden or a balcony as well. Usually people tend to leave those flats when they create a family and need a much bigger place. If you want to build a house, you should know the trade unless you have a skill to share or you have friends or admirers willing to do it for you. You can always start with those DIY house kits and develop it through years. You must apply beforehand to the local centre as some towns and cities have a restricted allowance on building new houses for various reasons."

"OK, I see. It all sounds fabulous and totally unreal," he said.

"Why? Isn't it the purpose of life? To be living freely and happily? And socially?"

"It just sounds impossible. Where I come from, this could only be seen in movies and I am sure if a movie showing what you said was released, the government would ban it to protect themselves. We believe, in my Island, that most people are not intelligent enough to make big decisions and we do everything in our power to keep it that way; some people are better educated and therefore are given more powers than the others. I already feel it is going to be difficult to tell my people about the world. I know we are now a democracy but still, the new government in place likes to govern of course and the unseen government might just destroy my report."

"I guess you had better make the best report you can. You know freedom is not just for the people but for the members of that government you are talking about. I am sure most of them will be happy working in the local centers. If they have new ideas, they can always put them to vote on the net and if they discovered something new, likewise, they can post it on the net to be trialed before being out. I mean they are loosing nothing."

"Are you kidding? They would be losing their superiority over the people! They would be losing their control over the people! Of course they won't give up so easily and most of us, back in the Island, believe in them so much," Tristan said.

'I need them to keep my power', I think he thought.

"Well, I hope they believe more in themselves than in others. I still find it strange that someone would need someone else to govern him, to tell him what not to do and do. It sounds like they need coordinators, or their parents all the time, as if they are kids. Maybe it is because I never knew my mother and my dad was very independent that I think this. Anyway, I always thought that governments were to represent people," I told him.

"Thank you JR, for all that. Earlier, you said that people prefer bingo or lotto than card games with money. I can understand the loss of interest if money has no value, but what about those winnings? You said something like 'at least they win something?'"

"Yes, indeed, Tristan. You see some items are rarer than others. What we have profusely is shared profusely, what is more limited but needed by all is shared equally and we, I mean humans, create alternative sources or we try to multiply those resources, without damaging the Earth of course. On the other hand for example, some Artists may prefer to organize lottery type prizes when they want to give away one or many of their creations. The item can be viewed by everybody interested, online of course, but if someone wants it, either the artist gives it to them or they enter a lottery type draw. Some people are fans and go there everyday. There are local places and online games. If a piece is liked by a certain number of people around the globe, then it goes to the International Gallery, usually nearest to where it was made, unless the artist has his own gallery. Tomorrow, we will pass by the 'Local Market' where you will meet Sheila. She is a well-known alternative fashion designer who had marked the last 40 years incredibly. She is considered to be one of the most famous fashion designers of Post-History. Many of her old items are in world galleries but she still creates one piece each month for the international online bingo.

What about I warm up the dinner, we are having spinach and mushroom lasagne, with some onion soup I made yesterday. Would you mind going to my indoor garden and fetching whatever you fancy to add to dinner? I can see you keep looking at the notes you took this morning. Is there anything else you would like to know tonight? You've already written so much in a day," I said.

"Indeed I think it is time to relax and eat a little now. I would love to know how the majority of the world has turned to vegetarianism, but I think Michael will be better able to tell me how it all started. However, something that I would like to know tonight is what are the Peacefullers you are referring to and what about those Vegetarian and Vegan Police and the forces?" Tristan asked.

CHAPTER V

Tristan didn't speak much over dinner, maybe because I didn't say much either. I washed the dishes and we sat near the fireplace. I offered Tristan a relaxant from the box but he said he would try later but would rather take some chamomile tea for now.

He installed his notebook on his lap and was tapping on the page with his pen as if to show me he was waiting for me to start again.

"The Peacefullers are people who make sure all is smooth and peaceful," I said, "they are everywhere, some wear green or blue uniforms but the majority are just doing other jobs in their usual fashion and intervene if something happens. You will recognize them as they all have a rainbow ring tattooed around their right index finger. If they don't have a right hand, they usually get tattooed on the neck. Some even go to the extent of tattooing a full rainbow circle around their necks. I have to say that it does look good. They need to show a Peacefuller identity card to intervene. The Vegetarian Police are the people who do the same as the Peacefullers but regarding the way animals are treated both in the wild and in the farms on the land. They have a white dove tattooed in between their right thumb and index finger. Hunting for example is forbidden since the Ivolution. Then there are the Vegan Police who take care of the sea creatures. They have a dolphin tattooed on their hand, or neck.

Every year during the Christmas holidays, we all complete a number of online surveys to see if we all want something to change, such as a law for example, that we have decided we don't find suitable anymore. Since the Ivolution, we need fewer and fewer laws. I think we have around 10 laws left at the moment. The first law is that no human is allowed to kill another human, the second law is that to kill an animal, you must do it bare handed and one to one, as equals. No weapons or traps are allowed. I think this will change soon. I wonder if by next year, it will not have joined the first law: no-one will be allowed to kill another human or an animal. The Forces are those who control the prisoners, usually arrested by the Peacefullers, the Vegetarian or Vegan Police. Actually most Forces are composed of Peacefullers, Vegetarian and Vegan Police officers, and members of the public who like to enforce peace, respect and freedom," I explained.
"So, it means you have a juristic system. How does it work?" Tristan asked.
"If someone does something wrong, for example steal a piece of art from somewhere or from someone, or has been caught hunting, he is denounced online with all the evidence proving the accusation. Some of the Peacefullers investigate as well and as much as possible. Everyone on Earth is allowed to participate in the online trial: it has to be fair. The accused is free but followed during the full trial which can last for years, Only when it is irrefutable that the person has committed the crime, do they receive their sentence. At the moment, those proven guilty are tattooed

with their crime: where it is tattooed depends on the people online. The accused also has to serve a social sentence, in whatever area needs extra work. At the beginning of Post-History, they used to work in factories. We were lacking staff there at that time, but with the progress in technology and mechanics over the past three decades, most popular items are made by machine now. Members of the forces guard them. If someone has committed something worse such as murder, it is the victim or those closest to the victim who suggest what punishment they deserve, which is given only with irrefutable proof, and agreed by an online majority."

"Well, that's a brief summary I guess. The juristic system is a big matter. Don't you have any judges?"

"We are all judges. People believe in fairness, people believe in 'I am not going to give, what I don't want to receive', people believe in free and peaceful humanity. Honestly, crimes are rare nowadays. The new generations are all well educated to maintain this peaceful free world. They are educated to be respectful of themselves and others but also to be responsible. I mean it's pretty normal, I guess, who would want to educate the new generations otherwise? We are not beasts, we are humans, spirits incarnated in flesh. And the old generations, well, they are too old to commit crimes. Can you guess what the new generations are into at the moment? I mean the 15-30s?" I asked Tristan.

"No, I can't."

"They believe and act upon their beliefs that the Sahara desert can be reversed into a big forest, like it is on the other side of the ocean. They grew up hearing that we successfully restored the weather from being very perturbed to 'normal' again and about how we succeeded in replanting the Tropical Forest…they believe they can do the same there. I actually think it's crazy. They are saying that a long time ago a pretentious civilization was living along the Nile and they deserted one of the biggest forests on earth in two millennia. I can't honestly say, because I'm not good at History, as you know, but they have found and are still finding many things, since the Ivolution…things that were hidden by the people in control, all over the planet. But in all honesty, I can't say if it's true or not."

"Wow, I would love to see that happening. Do you think I could arrange a stay somewhere where they have started this project?" Tristan asked.

"Of course, you are free and everyone is free. You just need to check when there are flights, and available seats. It should not be a problem as we have many flights a day and you can also book your hotel from the net: find which one you prefer, and check to see if they have space. Otherwise, you could go for more of an adventure. It's up to you: many inhabitants offer rooms. You have many choices."

"Excellent, thank you."

"Please don't rush into this Tristan as we already have a schedule set for next week. Would you like a copy?"

"Yes, that would be great JR, thank you."

It was getting late, and I could see Tristan starting to yawn. I filled my pipe with a little head of sleeping marijuana and asked him if he wanted a puff. He said yes.

"I've never tried it," he added.

"Just go very easy on it. You will enjoy it more if you just take a little bit at a time. At least, it will prevent you from coughing. Also, it will be better if you go straight away to your room or you might well fall asleep here" I advised him. Tristan took two small but deep puffs and said goodnight. I took Lou to the Crescent and when I went up to the bedroom later, I could hear Tristan snoring. I lit a nightlight candle, acknowledged the beautiful day that has passed.

"Thank You," I said out loud.

CHAPTER VI

After I recited the Reiki principles, I blessed my glass of water and recited my morning prayer: "May this New day be filled with Joy, Beauty, Peace, Respect, Freedom, Abundance and Love for everyone and every animal as it was yesterday and for ever and ever. Amen." The house was silent and I could hear the seagulls outside doing their morning reviews.

Tristan only came down after my morning walk.

"Good morning Tristan. Did you sleep well?" I asked.

"Good morning JR. I slept like a stone. I went up, changed into my night pajamas and fell onto the bed. I didn't move all night it seems and even didn't cover myself. I feel so refreshed, like new."

"Great to hear Tristan. Today is our last day in Brighton, tomorrow, as you know we will be going to London and then we are travelling. So today, we are going to the Local Market, you might want to see all the new fashions there, and honestly, you should get some stuff," I suggested.

"So, I just take all I want, I mean all I need" he smiled.
I smiled back.

"It is not so easy amigo," I said "all the common things are so abundant that you can have as many as you like. But honestly who needs more than 1000 spoons? And already that is a big number."

"Yes, but one may want thirty of that model, and thirty of that color and thirty of that shape. I mean you know," he pointed.

"And what is the problem? Do you like everything? Every color? Or rather, don't you find some things ugly and even find it shocking that others like them?"

"Yes."

"So, you see there are things for everyone. And if you just take what you need, in the types that you like, then you are leaving a lot behind for the others, aren't you?"

"I guess so," he replied.

"For products that are more special, where you will see designers and artists at their stalls, they will choose if they want to give you their creation or not. It is their choice. Some have plenty of same item but others only do one-offs…originals. So just wanting it is not enough but you can always play bingo if they refuse and you could get it online. Not to worry, most of them make things for the online bingo, as it is a great way to show yourself off. There is also an international market online, where each designer gives to the world. It depends what value they give their products. I am sure that all the artists of the world dream of having a piece exposed in international gallery even if many deny it. Shall we go? We'll walk there, as it is not too far," I asked.

"Yes, I'm ready. Thank you for the breakfast."

"Here, take some hemp bags."

"Why? I will use plastic carrier bags."

"We don't make such things."

"Ah, ok. Talking of bags, do you still collect the dog messes now in Post-History?"

"Of course we do Tristan with biodegradable hemp 'plastic' type bags that we put in the dog waste bins that are also lined with a bigger biodegradable hemp bag. It all gets collected and returned to the ground; usually put in holes in the soil as fertilizer. Recently, a company has started to incorporate living plant seeds mixed with the hemp of the bags. I think it is great. Wherever I put the mess I know something will grow. More food, that is and flowers. We only do this in towns, cities and villages. When we are out in nature, we usually toss it to the side of the pathway, leaving it to act as a fertilizer on its own. Are you doing the same back in the Island?"

"Oh, pretty much, yes. Although we have to collect it everywhere and we put it in a plastic bags that in turn go into the ground in bigger plastic bags."

"So you are telling me that the mess is in the plastic bags goes in other plastic bags, and then into the ground. Are the bags biodegradable?" I asked.

"Not that I know off. We like plastic," he confirmed.

"As do we, but biodegradable is more respectful to the planet. It seems to me that you stop fertilizing the earth in doing so, don't you? I mean the plastic takes so much more time to decompose than the waste, if at all, doesn't it?" I noted.

"We don't really care about fertilizing the soil. We just don't want to see it."

It was a fresh, sunny October morning without any wind. "Brighton is known as a World Creative City. There are five famous Creative cities around the globe. Kumasi, San Francisco, Chiang Mai, Sao Paulo and Brighton. They hold the best designer universities in the world. Most new ideas originate from those places. My dad moved to Brighton after the Ivolution to start in creative carpentry. I guess he wanted to escape the more traditional approach of my granddad who used to do copies of historic furniture. He met my mother here but she left him very soon after I was born, saying she had a career in front of her and she would not have any time for a family. My dad was heart-broken and has stayed alone ever since. He always assumed she left for someone else, although it has never been proven. We never heard of her anymore. I sometimes look on the Internet for her, but all the people with her name are not her."

"Oh, I'm sorry to hear that. I come from a very traditional family," said Tristan; happy we were also discussing private matters. "My parents are Christian Catholics in the traditional sense. They never separated, they were never allowed. Their faith forbids them. I don't think they've ever really been happy together, but I come from a rich family on both sides. And, well, their parents, really, decided on the wedding. Money needs to stay in the same hands, was the motto. I know, my mother had a little flirt with a poet from the town where she is born but he was not allowed in the family circle, and responsibility comes before love in my family. I can't tell you which is the saddest: my or your story. They both feel equally sad," Tristan pondered.

"I agree Tristan. Hey! Can you see that big building there and all the people everywhere around? Well, here it is."

"I have to say, I'm amazed by the amount of food growing everywhere, in all the parks, along each road, in streets, roundabouts, everywhere. It's absolutely amazing, the profusion of it all," Tristan said.

"Oh, yes, we have more than enough, and wait until you see the countryside. I mean it is incredible, really. Everyone is very pleased and the animals are very happy indeed."

"Well, I have to say; I like it all so far. I'm starting to feel very happy, happier than I've ever been. Although I still worry about my Island. The government won't be pleased. I may have to find a way to give the information to the general public but if it doesn't come from the top, they will believe it's a trap, a conspiracy. I don't know what to do."

"Let's not worry about that now. You will have plenty of time to think how to present the matter. I mean your journal is going to be pretty amazing."

"Yes. I know. I just don't want them to think it is pure fantasy. You know, science fiction or something like that. It is totally real and, unbelievable, unless you are in it."

"Well, I can't really understand your point. For me and I'm sure for many of us, it is unbelievable to live the way you told me you do back in your Island. I mean with government, money, diseases and those entire ridiculous restrictions. Anyway, here we are. Enjoy."

On the way to the alternative market, we passed by the spoon stall. Rashid was making a spatula. He is the best spoon carver I have met, incredible and a very good teacher as well. He's another one who totally lives a passion and is the best at it. I gave him the last three spoons I had made on my birthday to add to the 'help yourself' wooden spoon compartment. It looked like there was still one spoon from the 10 I gave last year. 'OK, that's not so bad', I thought. Tristan was looking around, touching fabrics, trying on tops he had never thought could exist.

"Tristan, honestly, enjoy. You have some of the best creators here. Don't be shy to talk to them. Ask if you would like something. As you can see, many products are labeled help yourself. If you'd like one or two or three or more, just take them, or ask them, but please be considerate. If you ever take too much you can always bring it back or if you have used them, take them to the used items sections of any market or second- hand shops and give them away there."

"Well, not to worry, I shan't take too much. My suitcase is already full and I can't post anything back to the Island as we are still closed to the world."

"OK. If you want to come this way, we'll go to the Alternative market where my friend Sheila is. You remember, I told you about her yesterday. I will stay there for a while and you can shop around. I'll meet you back

there."
"OK, great," he agreed.

As we entered the room, I recognized the music. Jon was at the decks with his strange style. He mixes every type of music that has ever existed in one single mix. Many people don't like it. They find they cannot dance to it but he always replies "It's not so much a style of music to dance to even if at some moments you may want to move, but music to work with, either at home, or in a workshop but also at markets, it works very well."

"People don't get bored of a song, it all goes too fast, and I like it. We used to play with Sheila, listening to his mix. You know like that program on TV where the participants need to guess the music track they are hearing. So we used to push our virtual button when we knew the answers. Sometimes it was such a laugh."

"Do you like the music?" I asked Tristan.
"Ummm, well, I'm not sure. It goes too fast and there are so many sounds. It doesn't sound continuous enough for me but it definitely suits the place. I mean those haircuts that some have got…wow! And the clothes! It's absolutely crazy."

"Hello Sheila? How are you doing?" I asked. Her head was still shaved, as always.
"Hey JR, great to see you here, my pal. It's been a while. You rarely come down here anymore. I miss the time you made clothes and worked here. Sebastian is popping around soon. Zoe is late." Sheila hugged me.
"You made clothes?" Tristan asked.
"Oh excuse me. Sheila let me introduce you to Tristan. Tristan, this is Sheila."
"Very nice to meet you Sheila. Do you mind if I look

around your stall? You have some pretty amazing things
here," Tristan asked.

"Please Tristan. It will be my pleasure," Sheila replied.

"Tristan comes from the closed Island in the south. He is
the first of his kind to have been out of his land. He is
discovering the world and is writing a report to give back to
see if they want to open their frontiers," I said quietly to
Sheila.

"Oh! Really. I heard it on the TV that something like that
was happening. I mean that there were movements on the
Island. I like his style, he makes me think of pictures of my
grandparents' time, back in History. So funny but he looks
so confident in them. It's lovely," she replied.

"Sheila, may I ask, do you have lots of these jackets, like the
one with the sparkling Jesus embroidered on the back and
front and with a heart on the sleeve? I love it. JR told me to
ask. You are the first person I am asking it and I am not
sure how to ask. Do I have to ask if I can have it or do you
put it at Bingo?" said Tristan.

"You can have this one if it fits, Tristan. It would be my
pleasure for you to have one of my creations," said Sheila.

"Really? Are you sure?" Tristan looked surprised.

"If I told you so. Come on, try it on. There is a mirror near
the steps just there if you want to see how it looks."

"You remember what I told you Tristan about Sheila. She is
a world famous designer. You should be so proud she has
given you one. I know people will be jealous. And it suits
you perfectly," I said to Tristan when we were by the
mirror.

"Thank You Sheila. I absolutely love it. And it suits me
perfectly. Thank you again," Tristan said.

"My pleasure," replied Sheila.

"Tristan, maybe you want to go and have a look around,

now you know how to ask," I smiled.
"OK, I'll do that. I'll be back here then. Is that OK?"
"Yes, like we said. I'll be here," I concluded.

Lou started to get excited with all the movements at the
market. He was showing me that he wanted to play. So I
decided to leave Sheila for a while and take Lou for a little
walk. I sat down outside in the park and I was dozing off
when I felt gentle vibrations in my pocket. At first I
thought it was my phone but it was that little stone I
collected on Saturday. I completely forgot it was there…I
hadn't worn these trousers since before the party.
"I hate her" I heard in my head.
"What?" I answered.
"I hate that women who had me recently."
"What is it? Sorry? Who's speaking?"
The voice was in my head but it didn't seem like it was
passing through my ears.
"I am the stone," I heard again. "I need to talk to you. You
have to help me."
I knew from my studies in parapsychology that this
phenomenon existed but it had never happened to me
before.
I am good at telepathy, we learned it at school but I rarely
use it, I prefer to use a phone. It feels more real, so I rarely
answer back in telepathy, I just receive the message. I prefer
to hear the voices of those who are contacting me.
"Well, you need to help me now that you have me," I heard
again.
"OK, what would you like me do?" I asked the stone that I
now was looking into.
"First I need to tell you a little story and then you will need
to do something for me. Is that OK?"
I could feel the stone pulsating in my hand.
"Well if you insist but that will depend on what you are
asking of course."

"I am so glad that the lace broke, honestly. That woman was horrible. I first belonged to a little girl and I liked that. I love to be seen and looked at because it took years to form myself and now that I was out I wanted to shine. Anyway, I was offered to that little girl and she didn't care about me at all. She didn't even use me around her neck. It was so sad. I used to love her but she could not hear me, and she attached me to her key ring. It wasn't so bad after all, she kept me and maybe over the years, she would have loved me but she lost me one morning and a woman picked up the key ring and never took it to lost property. She detached me and used me. She was an older woman, in her 70s, and she was trying to increase her power. She said she would have been glorious if this Ivolution never happened. She was using me to intensify her bad wishes on others, her controlling wishes on others. It was so tiring for me to try to block this bad energy. Of course I could not block all of it and one day the lace snapped. I was free again. And you found me."

"Hey, what a story little stone." I was stroking it, as if I felt its pain.

"The thing is she is pretty strong this woman and she wants me back in case I tell anyone. She is looking for me everywhere. I want you to connect with her, through telepathy, and disconnect her from me. Cut that connection please. When you have done so will you carry me around your neck? I am certain someone will love me, want me and I will tell you if I feel OK leaving you. Is that OK? Please. I can still feel her energy. Please do it or at least drop me back onto the ground so I can ask someone else. Please."

I didn't want to do it, but I agreed. I felt so much pity for the little stone. I focused, and holding the stone in my hand that was now hot and still vibrating, I connected with the woman. I did it in a way so she could not visualize my face...a hidden call. I thought that would be better: you never know with those types of people. If I were a

Peacefuller, I probably would have gone and seen the woman. But being me, I just did what the stone asked me. When the stone stopped vibrating, I went back to the market with Lou and picked up a piece of hemp rope to which I attached the stone. It was as though it was dead again.

Jon had stopped his set and now the disc jockey was playing some fast techno music mixed with guitars. Someone was singing on top of that. I didn't know them but they were pretty good and innovative. "I love this place," I thought.

I went back to sit with Sheila and we chatted while waiting for Tristan to come back. It's amazing the number of people from around the globe who know Sheila and come here just to visit her and ask her for a creation. She has a limited number each day and comes here once a week. She says she does three pieces a day, so 18 pieces a week. Two of her weekly productions go to online Bingo and one to the local bingo. She brings the rest here, to the market. Of course, like every other creator, she takes a picture of each new product that she makes and puts it on the 'new creation' website under the alternative fashion section for all who are interested. She still inspires many new designers around the globe.

Tristan came back with 2 bags full and a big smile.
"It's unbelievable this place, this world. Oh, I'm so excited. I feel like a teenager again."
We laughed. He was wearing the jacket Sheila had given him.

CHAPTER VII

"Tristan? I reserved a table for this evening for both of us at 'Jane's and Adam's', they came by the market earlier on and I thought it could be a good idea. Is that OK with you?"
"Sure" he replied entering the house.

Tristan went upstairs and I made myself a cup of chamomile tea.

When we were both ready and after I'd fed Lou and took him quickly out, we headed for 'Jane's and Adam's'. Tristan was still wearing Sheila's jacket but over a white t-shirt he had found in the afternoon, with the flag of our planet, the earth, printed at his front centre. I didn't change.
"JR, is it possible to pass by a chemist on the way?"
"I am not sure what you are referring to Tristan," I replied.
"A pharmacy."
"You want to go to the repair centre? Anything wrong?" I asked.
"Well just a chemist will do really; I need to pick up

something for athlete's foot. I've suffered from it since my childhood. I was a swimmer back then and the moisture didn't help."

"Oh, I see. Well, if you remember, I told you that we didn't have many ailments nowadays, and for the ones persisting, we use herbal remedies and nutrition that everyone knows about as we learn it at school. Can you wait before we go to bed, unless you want to do it now?"

"No, I can wait. It's OK for now but I can feel it starting again," he replied.

"So before bed, pour some apple cider vinegar on the infected area and let it dry. Some people prefer to prepare a footbath with the apple cider vinegar diluted in water. It is anti-fungal anyway and will help your cause for sure. It might sting if your skin is open but don't worry, it stops fast. Maybe do it also after each shower, as a preventive, if it is that bad."

"Thank you, I'll give it a try. Do you have some at home?"

"For sure. Everyone has it at home. It is so useful."

"Tristan, there are no menus here. They've done the same meal everyday for the last 20 years. They only serve dinner and for five tables, most for two people but there are two tables for four. They are well loved in the area. They grow everything they serve and they're always full."

"Sounds good. I am starving. I ate a bit this afternoon but there were so much to see. I also stopped for an energy joint at some point" he smiled.

We were starting on the soup when Suzie entered the restaurant followed by a very strong looking man.

"No way, look who's here! JR!" she screamed entering the room. I mean it always felt like if she was screaming, she had such a high voice. "Let me introduce you" she continued.

"JR, Mike; Mike, JR and you are?"

"This is Tristan," I replied.

"OK, nice to meet you Tristan. Well Tristan, Mike; Mike, Tristan."

"Hello."

"Hello," they both said almost simultaneously.

"Mike is the man I told you about on Saturday, you remember?" she asked me.

"Of course, I remember," I replied.

"He's getting ready for the Olympics next year. I won't qualify. Maybe the next one."

"Oh, wow, well-done" I said to Mike.

"Yeah, he is competing in boxing at the Trans-Olympics. Oh I hope he'll win. It will be in Miami. I would have preferred it to take place in another sport city but hey it has to be hosted in the same place. We can't do our own Olympics on the side. It would be so disrespectful."

"That's for sure. I mean it's great isn't it, that you guys have your own categories at the Olympics, even if it is not at the same time? I prefer to watch the Dope-Olympics: it's crazy how they break records with the dope they take. Of course I do respect the athletes and the records at the standard Olympics with no doping but hey, it's still fabulous that we can see how fast a human can run, don't you think? And with the help of dope," I added.

"Yeah, I watch it as well," replied Suzie. Mike was looking to sit down but kept smiling. Tristan was looking at us. His jaw had dropped.

"I'll be happy to know if Mike won or not, but I'm sorry I won't be watching it. Boxing is not for me," I said.

"Oh, you're so wrong. It's great to watch. I am really getting into it, even more now that I know Mike of course." Suzie stroked Mike's back.

"Well, you must be hungry and our soup is getting cold. Have a lovely diner. Nice to meet you Mike and all the best with your boxing," I said.

"OK, OK, we're going. See you later sweethearts and don't

worry about your house and plants! Tina or I will look after them" Suzie said, now pushing Mike to their reserved table.

"What's that all about?" asked Tristan as soon as they left us. "Trans-Olympics? Dope-Olympics? Is it what I think it is?"
"I think so. Trans-Olympics are the Olympics for Transsexuals and Dope-Olympics for the athletes who enjoy doping themselves," I explained.
"Oh my god! Well I don't have any god but hey, what? No way it can't be. No way, no way" Tristan shouted.
"Why not?"
"I don't know. It's not normal."
"Well, transsexuals have their own categories. At the end of the day, if those people are happier with a sex change, then it doesn't matter, does it? We just noticed they were not equal to the usual athletes, so we started their own Olympics. It doesn't last long as it is a minority on Earth. Regarding the Dope-Olympics, it's just great to watch and it's well supervised."
Tristan stopped talking for the rest of the meal. He looked very deep in thought. I left him to himself and didn't engage in any discussion but thought of my bag to pack for tomorrow and what I would want to take with me. 'I wouldn't need very much. I could always pick up some used trousers or a jacket if I needed it, that I could give back somewhere else. Or maybe some new stuff, if I really liked it. Well, we'll see. There are so many things everywhere I wasn't worried. Maybe I'll just take an empty bag, but actually why would I need a bag? I could always pick one up if I need one en route. OK, I'll take a small bag at least with toiletries for the evening and my two favorite shirts, the same for trousers, one pullover, a few pairs of socks and briefs and one hoodie. That should do and my mini portable computer and the headphones.'

'Do I have enough bags to collect Lou's mess? Yes, I do. Cool' I thought when I finished packing my bag.

CHAPTER VIII

After the first part of my morning routine, I drank my blessed glass of water and got up to get dressed, comfortably and warm. I always bless my first glass of water and last one of the day too. We know so much about the memory of water. And I believe by blessing it with Reiki energy and by telling it to purify me, energize me and fortify me it acts upon my asking. It's such an amazing thing, water. I heard they are experimenting on water communication, in the universities of the best cities of sciences.

Tristan was ready, and packed, waiting in the kitchen-dining room with his suitcase. He had changed his man handbag for a bigger bag pack. He also had a small bag attached to his belt. He was dressed back in his usual clothes.

"Good morning JR, did you sleep well? I'm sorry about last night. Anyway, do you think I could leave this suitcase at the airport and pick it up when I fly back to my Land?" he asked.

"Good morning Tristan. Yes, I slept well and no worries about last night. We'll stop at Gatwick on the way to

London and check if they have any boxes available. You probably need a padlock. We can collect one on the way to the station."

The train wasn't full early that morning. We sat in the first wagon on the seat facing forward. Tristan took his notepad from his bag and a pen.

"Can I use this time on the train to ask you more questions?" he asked.

"Yes, of course Tristan."

"Since I met you we've spoken together in English, isn't that right?"

"We have spoken in Igual, Tristan."

"In Igual? But it sounds so much like English"

"Because the band called 'The English' sings in Igual. I love their new single 'See you at the better end'. It's great. Have you heard it?" I asked.

"No, I don't know it. But it doesn't make any sense. Why…?"

"Why what?"

"Why isn't it the same name? Why isn't it called English anymore?"

"Well, I guess you'll have to ask Michael about that."

"Oh, I can't wait. There are so many questions I want to ask him." Tristan looked at the first page where a few days ago he wrote 'Marijuana is legal. It saved the planet'.

"Everyone around the globe speaks Igual and it is taught at school. Of course the elders don't all speak it, nor my dad's generation, but all of us, we do. We can learn many local dialects at school, if you're into it. Here for instance we speak Brits, it is a bit like Igual but we cut some consonants and change some. For example water becomes va'er. I assure you that visitors don't understand us," I explained.

We stopped at Gatwick and we were lucky, we arrived just as someone had left his box. We would have had to ask

Michael or Jasper if they could keep it for now; I don't like to ask this kind of favour. Tristan didn't know how long he would stay in the World before returning to his Island. I think he had up to 6 months to make a full report.

Once we were back on the train, Tristan started again. "Now, you said everyone, I mean almost everyone is vegetarian."
"Yes, that's true."
"How do you get your protein? Back in the Island, we are told that those who choose those types of diets lack so many things, such as proteins."
"I guess it is like a myth, completely unfounded," I replied.
"No, the government experts…"
"Sorry to interrupt you here Tristan, the government experts again? Them? What about all the other experts? Surely they cannot all be working for the government?"
"Euh, well, euh, the best experts we have work for the government."
"Really, according to who?"
"The government of course."
"Well, let me tell you that in the nutrition courses at school, we learn about all the food that is good for us. We study why it is good for us. Honestly, I don't remember too much of it but I do remember what to eat. There are plenty of foods high in protein. Hemp is one."
"We are not allowed hemp in the Island as you know."
"Maybe the experts are not so wrong then, if all the good food is banned."
"Or modified" Tristan added.
"Sorry Tristan, modified food?" I was surprised.
"Yes genetically modified food."
"What! Why?"
"For the fruits to look nicer, or bigger for example. All our produce has to be seedless. What is the point of them having seeds? I agree with that."

"What? You are growing food and getting rid of the seeds? Now then, you're not joking, are you? I have to say it is terrible. Why do you do this? Seeds are great. They are wonderful. They bring Life. What is the problem with them? You can even eat them. They are so good for us. Oh, dear, it is so sad." I felt tears in my eyes.

Tristan was looking very confused now. He looked like a schoolboy from an old picture of History. I felt pity. He didn't know what to say.

I took one of my study books and started reading, leaving Tristan in his confusion. What could I say to make him feel better? I needed to distract myself from these hell-like pictures I had in mind.

We arrived at London Bridge station and walked to Michael and Jasper's apartment. What a place they have! Overlooking Tower Bridge, on two floors with a garden. They have three cats, Holly, the eldest, Ben, the black one and Pussy, the smallest and youngest. None are related. In fact Ben belongs to Michael and they rescued Holly. Pussy had come in recently and doesn't want to leave anymore. They asked the Vegetarian Police if they had any record of a missing cat like Pussy, but until now, they'd only had no for an answer.

Jasper was alone waiting for us.

"Welcome guys and sorry, Michael was called to cover a class. He won't be long. You must be Tristan. Please, treat this like your home. Be comfortable. Would you like some tea or coffee? Michael told me you were staying for two nights. Where are you going after? Can I ask?"

"Yes we are going to the south. Tristan must meet Habibi," I replied.

"For sure. Is the report going good?" Jasper asked.

"Yes there are many things to tell," Tristan said at last.

Jasper came back carrying a tray with a coffee pot and three cups, a mug with milk and some dark sugar.

"Soya, isn't it Jasper?" I asked, knowing that was always their favorite.

"As ever," he replied smiling.

"So Jasper, may I ask. What do you do?" asked Tristan.

"I am an accountant Tristan."

"Really? How can you be an accountant if there is no money? Is it to do with the card games?"

Jasper laughed out loud.

"No I work in the London stock market. We are a big distribution center for all the land around and we export all that we over produce here. It is non-stop. We are in continuous relationships with all the other distribution centers: New York, Berlin, Jerusalem, Hong Kong, Dubai, to name a few, as well as those inland like Manchester and Portsmouth. We are very connected with the coordinators as well."

"So you are still in numbers?" said Tristan, trying some humor.

Jasper laughed again.

"Yes but we have tonnes, kilograms, stones, potatoes or bananas or whatever we are counting written after the number instead of a symbol at the front, like it probably is where you come from." He was still laughing.

"Well, it makes sense. Could I come with you tomorrow and see where you work. I think it would be very interesting if I made a fuller report on this matter." Tristan was curious.

"Of course, it's alright Tristan. I'll be there from 6am to 10am. That is my daily shift."

"So early, and so few hours?" Tristan observed.

"At the stock exchange that is. Afterwards I usually work from home on the computer, I also coordinate. But that it is not my only job. I chose those hours. You see I sleep 5 hours at night and I take a siesta at 1pm for a couple of hours. I am a trumpeter. I practice every evening from 5 to

10 and I play in a concert on Wednesdays and Saturdays at different venues around London. We even played in Edinburg not so long ago. In the spring, we also play on a Sunday morning, outside in the park with the Orchestra." Jasper was smiling and drinking slowly from his tea. Tristan was looking at his page where he was writing while listening.

"Tonight we are playing a repertoire from Vivaldi including the Four Seasons. Your seats are reserved for tonight's show, a private balcony overlooking the orchestra."
Tristan stopped writing.

"It starts at 8pm," added Jasper, "before that, I think Michael wants to take you both to a new restorative house concept that just opened. It seems like fun. Every table has a mini garden incorporated in the centre and you pick up all that you want from it. Although they also present a card of meals that are home cooked, it's very experimental from what I've heard. All the juices are homemade and they brew their own beers and make their own wines. It's starting to become a chain and they've opened another one recently in Warsaw. I think they have opened seven so far around the globe. It started in the creative city of Kumasi and worked almost instantaneously. It is outdoor, inside a big garden from which we can also pick up all we want. It is heated: the atmosphere is magical with fireplaces everywhere, statues half covered with moss, streams, lanterns and soothing relaxing music that introduces guests to a variety of traditional and modern music from each part of the world. I think Michael said the reservation was for 5pm. It is very close to the theater where I'm playing tonight."
"Thank you," said Tristan "I'm looking forward to all of this."

"There! I can hear him. Michael is here," said Jasper, getting up from his seat in the direction of the entrance corridor.

CHAPTER IX

"Chan has just won at the world bodybuilding championship. He just called me on my mobile. Can you believe it?" said Michael to Jasper.

"Ris'an is ni, s'ra'e o! He looks sur'rised a al'os every'hin I say. H's veird," Jasper replied to Michael as they were approaching the lounge. Tristan was trying to understand what he'd just heard.

I could see Michael was still going to the gym. What a body! And with his long black curly hair, he looked like a warrior from the cartoons I read when I was a child; a very beautiful man indeed. His skin is a little tanned just enough to show that he comes from the southern parts.

"Nice to meet you Tristan" Jasper said, stepping in front of Tristan offering him his large hand to shake. He looked almost twice the size of Tristan: like a hero from a cartoon in front of someone who has come from the old school boy pictures. That was very picturesque.

"Very nice to finally meet you indeed," said Tristan with a small trembling voice.

Jasper and Michael both laughed.

"Don't' be scared," said Jasper to Tristan, "he's built like a god and has a heart of a dolphin."

They both laughed again. Everyone sat down apart from Jasper who excused himself.

"Anybody want burgers and chips?" he said.

Tristan looked up at him, his eyes widened.

"Beef burgers?" he said. He looked almost as if he was biting on something.

"No, sorry we have bean or mushroom burgers? I usually serve with tomato sauce, fresh tomato slices and soya-melting cheese…we love soya in this house. Fresh spinach leaves as well, and I often add a spoonful of grains and seeds. Do you want me to add a spoon of hemp protein as well, in yours Tristan?"

"I've never eaten those types of burgers before. What are they made of?" asked Tristan.

"I think they also use eggs in their preparation. Do you want me to pick up the box for you to read the ingredients? Michael, I'll add some spirulina in yours, do you want a protein milkshake as well sweetheart?"

"Yes, that would be lovely love," said Michael to Jasper, "and some beans please."

Tristan opted for a mushroom burger with added hemp protein.

"Do you have mayonnaise?" he asked Jasper.

"No but I can make some, it's easy."

"Really, how you do it? Can you tell me?"

"Yes, sure Tristan. In a blender, you add 125ml of vegetable oil with 50 ml of soya milk, then the juice of half a lemon and half a tablespoon of mustard, salt, pepper. You blend it all together and then pour it into a small jar with a lid on it: that way it will last at least a week in the fridge. I think the quantity should be enough for you to have some for the few days you are here, I can always do more."

"You don't add any eggs?" asked Tristan while copying the recipe into his notebook.

"No, that's the recipe we follow at the moment. We love it. If you find a better one, please let us know. I'm always on the lookout for better tasting home food recipes. Thank you Tristan. That would be great. Look at Michael, the big lump I need to take care of, as chief of the kitchen. JR, I'll do your favorite," Jasper said leaving the room.

"So, Michael?" Tristan now turned to Michael, ready to write and start his questioning.
"Yes, Tristan," replied Michael.
"I'm sure there's no need for me to be introduced. You know where I come from."
"Yes, indeed Tristan." Jasper smiled, "and it is a pleasure to meet you. It feels like meeting someone from the past, from the last chapter of History. It is actually incredible and fantastic. I feel totally honored."
"I am well present, Michael. I assure you that where I come from there are thousands like me. We are not from the past, we live in the present."
"Oh, I'm sorry Tristan. I surely didn't want to upset you. I'm sure you understand what I'm saying. Again, I'm sorry. It is a real pleasure to have you here and I will be very glad to answer all your questions."
"Thank you," said Tristan. "Apologies accepted. So you're a history teacher?"
"Yes, that's right. I love it. This is my only job, although I help at the local communal garden and in the food growing boxes along the road at the front and back of the house, and I am the gardener of the house. I also take care of the wood for the central fireplace. I like to help on the weekends with the city wood supply service. There are no homes without a fireplace! I specialize in, approximately, the last 200 hundred years of history and I am a Peacefuller as you can see." Michael was showing his massive rainbow ring tattoo around his finger. He added: "I used to belong to the 'Bonding Lights', an elite force within the

Peacefullers who make sure no one is conducting nasty experiments, or active projects that would interfere with Life as it is; people who might create illegal weapons for example. But over the years, I calmed down a bit," he smiled, "although they still call me once in a while, mostly to know how I am these days. This is a force that doesn't have much to do any more, now that everyone feels responsible for Life. But hey! We never know. I would be happy to join a big operation if one comes our way."
"Oh OK! Great! I mean I sure know all that happened in the word before we closed our frontiers to the world."
"October 1998" said Michael.
"Yes indeed. The 17th of October 1998. We have a national commemoration day of the events, what a glorious day it is, the day we closed ourselves from the sinful world around us" added Tristan.
Michael was looking at Tristan straight in the eyes.
"So you want to know what happened?" he asked Tristan.
"Sure I do," replied Tristan. "I have noted many things since I arrived. JR has told me how the world is but he is rubbish at History, no offence JR!"
"No offence taken." I smiled.
"I want to know how it started, how it changed itself to this."

Jasper came back with a plate for each one of us.
"You OK guys? Eating on the sofas or do you want to sit at the table? I'm going to eat in my room, I want to finish some stuff on the computer before siesta. You don't mind guys? And I am not sure I want a History lesson as a table conversation to be honest."
"Yes, no problem Jasper" Michael and I said. Tristan looked like he didn't like the idea of having the plate on his knee where he had his notepad.
"Shall I bring you the bed-table, Tristan? It will be much more comfortable for you to write."

"Yes please" replied Tristan "thank you very much Jasper that would be very helpful if we are eating here." He didn't look like he liked the idea. But, it was good for him to be pushed a bit I thought, and I'm sure Michael and Jasper thought the same, to make him see new dimensions he'd never experienced.

"I've never eaten on a sofa, like this" Tristan finally admitted. "On a bench, outside, yes, sometimes, but I don't sit on the floor to eat. We don't do this in my family, it's for the lower classes. And on the sofa? Surely it causes indigestion. I don't think people do this, eating on their sofas."

Jasper and Michael were looking at him surprised. And then they burst out laughing. I caught the laughing too and we could not stop for at least five minutes.

It was so funny, what looked like a schoolboy from a History picture, telling us everything he is not allowed. I wanted to ask him: 'Do you enjoy life at least? I mean are you allowed?' but I preferred to keep my mouth closed. I didn't want to upset him. He looked so different.

"Jasper comes from what you probably know as Ireland" Michael finally said.

Tristan seemed relieved. Someone was talking to him the way he knew.

"Oh really? Which part?"

"The south, near Killaloe" replied Michael. "We go there every summer for three weeks to his family home. We stay with his parents and all his brothers and sisters. It is a big house that they have there, 11 bedrooms. They use it for family gatherings. It belonged to their ancestors and has stayed in the family right until now, through the Ivolution. They still have paintings of their ancestors on the walls and other pictures. We love it there. It's so green and fruitful at this time of the year. We also go there for Christmas. This Island is the best place to go for Christmas. That is were

Ivolution started back in 2012 of your calendar. His family comes from all the corners of the globe for the events."
Jasper was now leaving the room.
"OK, here we start. I am off guys. See you later."
"Bye bye, sleep well" I said to him.
Tristan didn't bother and just smiled, with a 'I don't want to be disturbed, it is getting interesting' type of attitude.
"Rest well sweetie" said Michael. "We'll be a while downstairs. We are not going out. JR, are you staying?"
"Yes" I replied, "I would love to listen. I am not going to take any notes and I probably won't remember a lot but I'm sure I will know more than what I do now about History. Can I have some grass?"
"Of course JR, let me fetch the box. It is here on the shelves. Tristan you want some?"
"Oh, no. Not now. I'm working and want to focus. I don't want to miss anything."
"I'll have a puff or two JR," said Michael, giving me the box.

Tristan came back to his first note and wrote near year 0:
'2012. Ireland. It started.'
"So what happened?" asked Tristan.
Michael took 2 consecutive puffs and said:
"Early December 2012, a book came out. Habibi had arrived. I don't know if you are aware but after your Island closed, the world connected more and more with the help of the internet."
"Oh, yes, I guess so. We have the same in the Island, our own Internet communications, blocked from any other web."
"Well here everyone slowly got connected to it and shared ideas, pictures, videos, thoughts, theories, moments of their life, music, discoveries, new designs, philosophies."
"Yes, it is the same on the Island."
"OK, but in 2012, in your calendar. The man, I mentioned,

Habibi, advertised his book on the web. He had grown a small community of friends but it was enough to spread the word fast. He never dreamed that his book would spread so fast, everywhere. It was like a fantasy book, depicting a different world, a different type of social organization that would help humanity to survive the dark plans of those who were in control in his book."

"You mean it all started from a book?"

"Officially yes, but about 5 years before, Habibi and many others around the globe were already talking about the possibility of a New World, a better world for all. There were many versions, many theories, much nonsense also and many great causes. But Habibi was special. He didn't belong to any form of control. He didn't belong to any political party or religion, or group. He didn't even grow up in a city but in a mountain. His dad was a carpenter and his mother a mid-wife in the local town. They didn't belong to the privileged of the world but with the people. He was an individual and still is, free from boundaries and barriers, free like a bird. And he loved humanity and the world so much that he wanted a version where everyone would be happy: rich and poor, blacks and whites, gays and bisexuals, disabled people, everyone and every animal. He started to write things like 'why are all the public places seeded with unfruitful plants and Christmas trees?' It was always like a shock when he opened his mouth. He had suffered from it all his youth. Do you want me to take a break Tristan?"

"Just give me 2 minutes Michael until I finish writing what you just said, thank you."

"OK, no problems. JR can I have some more please?"

I was just starting to fall asleep when I heard Michael asking.

"Oh, sure Michael. Here is the ashtray. I left it. It is so strong. I can't finish it."

Michael smiled. Tristan was just finishing writing. I don't think he realized what just happened.

"Yes, he was talking of a transformation of the organization of society and not a destruction of some kind like so many theories at the time. One of the worst theories was that there were far too many people on Earth and that for it to survive, at least two-thirds of the population would have to be killed. Horrible, isn't it? Would you believe in killing two-thirds of the population?"

Tristan didn't reply at first. He was still taking notes.

"Over-population" he said at last.

"Over-population is what the people in control wanted them to believe but like Habibi said, there is a limited number of souls. 'How can you be so pretentious to say that you are creating more souls? You can only create bodies for the souls, Humans! And all souls can be incarnated at once!' No, it was over-concentration that happened on Earth and limiting all the resources made it even more difficult for everyone except the rich at the time. No, one of Habibi's many advantages was that his version was the only one which gave total power to the people and not to a small group of people, whoever they may be: liberals, different religious groups, capitalists... Some theorists were hiding a form of control behind their beautiful visions, so many didn't believe in Habibi at first, until that book. It showed a world were everyone would be free and happy and in control. Oh. That wasn't that easy at first. You know, there were times when demons hid behind plastic beautiful faces and big smiles, actors really everywhere."

"Just be Real," I said out loud. But it seemed as though no one heard.

Michael carried on: "Many people, religious or not and priests who involuntarily wanted the destruction of most humans, believing in just a small bunch of survivors or selected few, called Habibi a 'false-prophet'. The straight people and frustrated ones didn't like the fact that he protected the gays and transsexuals, the rich, the poor and vice-versa. The Buddhists pointed out that Buddha said 'Life is suffering' to which he replied 'if that is what you want to believe then that is what you create'. The Hare Krishna were singing 'Hare Krishna'. Only the alternative people, the Indians and the Muslims didn't know what to make of him. He had origins in the north of Africa, speaking in your way Tristan but lived in Europe when it all happened. The Christians were confused after Habibi pointed out that 'if they were true followers of Christ, they should have refused money; not for poverty, but for freedom like Christ had asked them to. And of course to love one another as he prescribed, meaning to love everyone whatever their beliefs, their culture, race or sexuality'. The atheists liked him but wanted him to remove any connections or any writings on the source and the creation of the world and history he had spoken about. He told them that if they wanted to believe they were monkeys, that was their choices but they should know that monkeys are vegetarians and also that it explains why all the ones that believe in this ridiculous theory were so bad at making love…like monkeys, he used to laugh. Meanwhile, each and every one was realizing that he was providing a solution for the world. Some were saying 'we don't need a savior', but the terms 'prophet', 'savior' came up in every paper.

The governments exposed him the following May, trying to ridicule him, in public.

'What is it that you want?' they asked him publicly. It was on every channel, everywhere, like the Olympics. 'Do you want to be a king? Do you want to take the place of our kings? Of our presidents? Do you think you can be the king of the world? Look at yourself, bald, skinny, and hairy. Look at our charming princes. They look like kings!' Many were mocking him.

Habibi replied: 'No, this is not what I want. If I am a king, then all of you are kings and queens unless you are angels.' Both Michael and I said this together: it was so well known, even I knew it.

"'I just want to be left in peace'" carried on Michael, "'to be able to afford a house where I want and live near my family with animals and friends, knowing that everyone including all the animals around the planet are happy, comfortable and free, like they should be. Otherwise I can't sleep. You can call me any names you want. I have already been called a black beast up to Mithrad to name a few. I have just done what I was meant to do. That's all and I certainly can't afford plasticizers and new teeth to look nice in pictures.' Everyone that heard him was laughing at him at the time," said Michael.

"'When I was a teenager, I met a medium in Zwolle who told me that in this life I would again understand everything. I didn't know what she meant back then. But she said, 'you must not do what you did in your similar incarnation back in Morocco. Last time, you could not speak, no one wanted to know, and you went off to let yourself die in the desert. This time, I am sorry but no. You will try to kill yourself again and you might succeed but you are here to say all that you know. It is important. That is why you are here.'

'He is mad' the unbelievers were saying. 'He is here' the believers and new believers were saying.

He didn't make any sense of what she said at this time and he chose a life of personal degradation. The more he encountered the world, the more he suffered, the more he destroyed himself, drugs, sex, lack of food, smoking, dehydration. The more they destroyed life, the more he destroyed himself, as if they were in symbiosis. Everything that would help him 'sleep' faster. He caught many diseases and was kept alive by drugs from the medical businesses who were developing treatments but no real cures at that time. Everyone had to be a client. It was big business. Habibi was raped in his late childhood, early teenage years and never told anyone until before he thought he would soon decease. He actually used to come back to those men as he felt that was the only place where real love existed between men. It was sad to hear all that. We have made a movie of his life before the Ivolution. Do you want to see it Tristan, maybe tomorrow night? We are busy tonight."

"Yes, Thank you. Maybe I can even get a copy to take back with me. Can I get a copy of that Book too?"

"Of course, you can Tristan. I'll bring you a new tomorrow. Do you want more copies?"

"Oh, no. One of each is perfectly fine. Thank you Michael."

"Anyway," Michael continued, "The year before he wrote that book, he was taken very ill and was hospitalized. They saved his life: the doctors, the treatments and his friends who had found him practically dead in his bed. He had stopped taking treatment for the previous two years. Here we are, he did it again, tried to kill himself. It was so sad to hear. I still find it painful and I'm so grateful to him today that he helped the world become such an extraordinary place as it is today. Finally, his Book came out."

I felt my mouth was becoming very dry and I asked if anyone fancied a cup of tea.

"May I have a lavender tea?" asked Michael.

"Sure, you can" I replied, taking with me the dirty plates back to the kitchen. "Tristan?"

"Just a glass of water please JR, that would be perfectly fine. Thank you."

Tristan didn't stop writing all the time Michael talked. He was still writing when I left the kitchen and was still writing when I came back. Michael was filling a pipe: "Would you mind fetching some scones, JR. they are on the kitchen table. Jasper made them earlier on."

"With pleasure" I replied.

"And help yourself to fruit Tristan," Michael added.

"I'm fine. Thank you" replied Tristan.

"FINE: Fucked up, Insecure, Neurotic, Emotional, F-I-N-E, that is what my Reiki teacher used to say," I said when leaving the room again.

CHAPTER X

"Michael, you said that the guy, Habibi, saved the world with a book" said Tristan.

"No, he didn't save the world. He showed the world which direction to take if everyone wanted to be happy and free. It is the people who save themselves, and Marijuana saved the earth like JR told you for sure."

"Surely, a book is not enough?" replied Tristan.

"Why would you think so Tristan? Look at all the religions; each is based on a book, isn't it? Or a translation of a book. A book can be very powerful indeed. Look what a book did in 1940 of your calendar in Germany with that small bad man they had at the time…I can't remember his name, sorry," said Michael.

"Yes, I know whom you mean. We study his book at our private schools" said Tristan.

"Are you aware that those who are said to have helped end that war, were the ones that helped that man build his army and government to attack? Of course the people didn't know either. But the ones who gave the orders for war knew perfectly. It was to install and expand their hidden empire."

I had absolutely no clue who or what they were talking about. I understand that it is Michael's business to know but the rest of the world? What I don't understand is why would we learn the name and dates of the bad people the earth has seen? Why should we learn the horrible events the world has witnessed? No, you don't do that if you want a peaceful world. They move in the history memory bins, for most people. We keep the best: the truth and the arts.

"You have to remember Tristan, at the end, it was difficult times for the people. Most of them could not afford rent, let alone buy a property with their wage. Most of them either relied on the system to pay some of their rent or asked the banks for loans. They were not allowed to live in trucks, in empty houses nor in tents, unless in campsites. They were not allowed to make fires to keep warm in winter. It was very hard to live on earth really."

"Yes, I remember. That is why we closed our frontiers to the world, to protect ourselves from what was starting to happen" Tristan agreed.

"The governments and corporations that owned them controlled everything, from the toilet paper people used, to the media that the people were continuously harassed with. Many people, at the time, didn't really see what was happening, what those greedy people wanted to do, what they were doing to the planet through the help of everyone who were led to believe they were doing the best. Do you remember Tristan? They used to believe the lies. The people of some nations even believed the greedy ones on their thrones were blessed by God. I mean maybe they were blessed, because they were born into those families, but surely God didn't like them killing people in order to be more powerful, or have anyone killed to be more powerful. Isn't it how they built their powers, those families? Asking the poor and not so poor to go to war to expand their kingdom? Sometimes they would send one of their own to war, if it was really necessary, but it was always for their own glory. The people were lied to: stories, always stories. By the way, most movies from History have been remade to tell the truth. They used to give some privileges to their followers but never as many privileges as they had themselves. I mean they didn't have to wait on a rainy day for a bus to go to work in a desperate place with a very small wage, did they? They didn't have to wait in traffic, did they? No! Their demons, their protectors; I mean people from the people who would have given their life to save a member of any of those greedy families, one has to be completely dumb or programmed to accept such a stupid and demoniac task. No! They would clear the way with their cars and bikes with flashing lights.

Those families on their thrones were way above everyone and they wanted more, always more. The princes were becoming even greedier than the rest of their ancestors. Can you believe they even enjoyed being carried around on wooden thrones by blacks like in the slave times?"
"All that sounds like it is in the Island! It's what we revolted against recently. Because we wanted a democracy, we arrested our regents. Of course the new government is pretty much like the old one. I mean people have to have a government. I still can't really understand how it can work without one. People are stupid and we make sure they are programmed to be so," Tristan pointed out.
"Either you believe in The Source, what some may call God, representing all of Life or you believe in those who proclaim they have power over everyone or everything. You see Tristan; even Atheism was taught to program the people to believe in those in control. If one stops believing in a higher deity power then one will start believing in a higher human power and now that they had the power, they didn't need people to believe in a religion anymore, a religion installed to program fear and submission into people. This

is the opposite of the Source of all creation, really, the opposite of Love. It seems that you still believe in the second option, in those who proclaim they have power over everyone or everything? I guess it is normal. It happened here too at the beginning with the wealthy families like yours," said Michael. "They were so scared, but Habibi's vision was by far the best for the wealthier ones too. They could keep owning their properties and land, to a certain extent, to be fair. At least, with Habibi's version, there were no rebellions, no revolts and nor would they be needed afterwards either. It was to be Peace forever and they could keep their favorite houses."

"Oh, I see. But surely in many places, people want a big house, a big mansion, a big castle, don't they?" said Tristan smiling, expecting Michael to say something that would destroy the fairytale.

"Would you like to live in one of them?" Michael asked Tristan.

"I live in one of them back home, you should know, a 17th century mansion. I inherited it when my granddad died."

"I guess you must have gardeners and cleaners and servants, don't you Tristan?"

"Well of course Michael, I have all of them. How could I do otherwise?"

"Yes how could you do otherwise? Would you stay in your mansion if no one wants to do your garden? Or clean your windows? Or brush your teeth? Sorry, I am only joking there. You understand what I mean, don't you Tristan? When you can't pay them? Unless they need one of your skills in exchange or otherwise they would have to truly love you to do that for you," Michael said staring at Tristan. Tristan didn't say a world. He even didn't look up from his notepad. I'm not sure but I think he was starting to cry.

"I'll probably get a much smaller place indeed."

"Sorry?" Michael and I asked. We could hardly hear what

he just said.

"I'll probably get a much smaller place," Tristan said louder.

CHAPTER XI

"Hey guys, it is 4 o'clock!" we heard Jasper saying, when he was coming down the steps. "Michael, did you call the chimney sweep? I've just remembered," he added. Michael nodded a yes.

"Maybe you should get ready, or Michael, call the restaurant to make it five-thirty at least. I'm off, I need to join the group, we are rehearsing before the concert. I hope you all had a lovely chat. Am off! Am off, bye bye, bye bye bye."

I got up, grabbed my bag and went to the washroom to change. Michael left for his room. Tristan didn't move, as though he was transfixed in thought. It did not take me too long and I went straight down to show Tristan the bathroom.

"I'm fine," Tristan said, "I'm not going to change. My clothes are fresh from this morning. I feel like myself, the way I'm dressed. I'm sorry, I hope it won't be inappropriate but I'm happy like that. I am just going to use the toilet."

"It is perfectly fine. If you're happy like that, we're happy that you are like that" I smiled. "No worries, you can come as you want, with a blue Mohican if you like or large earrings! It's all absolutely fine. Actually the more dressed-up, the better, don't you think Tristan?"

"I'm not sure," he replied, "It scares me. It feels very sinful to let anyone dress the way they like. In my Island, we accept very few extravagances in the clubs or so, yes, but definitely not in the streets or in the office. People need to look nice."

I didn't reply. I didn't know what to say, quite frankly. He just sounded completely absurd. It felt like everything he was telling me about his Island was the opposite of Life. I can't understand how thousands upon thousands accept that reality, really. It's like being forced to be a 'dead' servant, the same that has happened throughout History. I thought of Habibi and how hard it was for him in those times. How did that guy survive those times, knowing all that he knew, with the understanding and the vision he had of the world and of God? How? I was impressed. All that I heard today from Michael made me love Habibi even more and I'm so glad and honored that I am going to visit him. I have never been yet; I don't like those big queues. But I promised myself I would go one day of course: no one should miss an event like that.

CHAPTER XII

The house was silent when I woke up. I knew Tristan and Jasper were out at the Stock Exchange offices. Michael was probably at the gym.

I did my usual routine and decided to take Lou out into town and have breakfast outside.

I walked along the Southbank. It was a lovely morning again; I was sure I'd be able to eat outside somewhere, they usually provided blankets in these months. It would be so nice to be out in the fresh air, drinking a hot cup of tea, feeling comfortable and warm, overlooking everybody on their way to or from work, or whatever activities they were doing. I stopped at 'Breakfast & Grass'. I love this chain. It started in Brighton and had now expanded everywhere. Some say it originally came from Amsterdam, but we can't be sure. There were no companies named as such when it started, but some say that the concept already existed but was integrated into an all-meal type of offer. Anyway, they only do breakfast and grass. And it was the perfect place to start a day like this one, where I will spend most of the day listening to Michael telling Tristan how it all happened. I was interested of course, now that I'd heard what he said yesterday, I wanted to hear the rest, but honestly, what did he say yesterday that would make me want to change anything from life as it is today? Absolutely nothing. We are all so happy and free. It seems truly unbelievable that all that happened…I mean I know, it did happen. Habibi is here and we are only year 40 but it is still very strange that the people of those times accepted it all. I will see if Michael enlightens me on that matter later today.

"Good morning Michael" I said when I entered Jasper's and Michael's kitchen.
"Good morning sweetheart" he replied, "did you sleep well?"
"How could I sleep badly?" I replied, "Everything is perfect."
He smiled and gave me a hug.
"Well I'm making some rice with beans; it is my protein plate after workout. I always add a teaspoon of hemp protein as it contains all the essential amino acids. Do you want some?"
"Oh, no. Thank you Michael, I just ate at 'Breakfast & Grass', I'll make myself an orange juice."
"Cool. I've made some already. I can't function without orange juice in the morning," he said.

We were sitting at the kitchen table when Jasper and Tristan came back. Both were smiling although Tristan looked like he didn't sleep at all.
"I'm feeling completely knackered," said Tristan. "Do you mind if I go for a nap. I hardly slept last night. There's so much going on. I couldn't stop thinking. I am exhausted."
"Good morning Tristan," replied Michael, "please do. Do you need anything to drink or eat beforehand?"
"I can't, I'm too exhausted. Excuse me please."

Jasper sat at the table with us.

"Oh dear, he is so bizarre" he finally said. "Every time he met new members of staff, he asked so many questions. Trying to understand how everything can work without money. Asking them if they would not rather be paid to work so they could be more privileged than others."

Michael laughed. I was livid.

"You know what each of them replied to him? 'And why should I get paid for something I enjoy doing, and that is profitable to humanity. Excuse me but your question doesn't make sense. To be more privileged than others? Are you out of your mind? I have the house I love, the family I love, the friends I love, and every food I love in abundance. I travel as much as I like and everywhere that I like. What are you talking about?' Some were saying 'I party every night and come here to work before I go to bed. I only give one hour here per day.' He never knew what to reply but obviously he's been thinking a hell of a lot during the night."

Michael and I were not surprised by the replies. I guess we would have said exactly the same thing if he would have asked us.

We decided to move to the living room where we lit the fireplace, took the relaxing box and sat on the sofas. We chatted until early afternoon, listening to some new music. Jasper wanted to watch a science fiction movie, Michael a period drama but I told them that Tristan could come down any minute and we would have to stop the picture to carry on the lesson. So we agreed on music instead.

"Hey, do you want to listen to the 3Gs?" Jasper asked, "I got their new album few days ago."

"I can't believe you have it" I replied, "Moonja, my youngest cousin, is in it. They were looking for a new member and he applied. He really hoped they would like his style, his talent. We knew at the auditions that it would work out pretty good for him. He is perfect for the band. I'm going to see him play at the winter Muktor festival…I can't wait, I'm so excited. Do you know what 3Gs stands for, Jasper?"

"Guitars, Gigs and Girls. Everybody knows that JR. They won at World-Factor, didn't they, a few years ago?"

"So your cousin is in it?" continued Jasper. "Do you think he could get me a few passes for the next concert in London. I'm a big fan of the band and I am not the only one! They are packed out almost every night."

"I'll do my best Jasper. But you better tell me which date you prefer before I'll contact him."

"OK, I'll go and have a look at my calendar, their dates and venues later and let you know."

"Great. Can you believe I am also going to see Michael? The Michael. He will be performing his new album. I've never seen him before. I love him. I think he's the best-known singer on Earth. He truly looks like an angel. Some say he is the re-incarnation of another Michael who came in Habibi's youth," I said.

I looked over at Michael who didn't seem very enthusiastic about joining Jasper at the event.

"I don't like those big crowded events," he said, "I need to have space around me to breathe, and the queues at the toilets, nope sorry. It's just not for me."

CHAPTER XIII

Tristan came down early afternoon. He looked a bit better.
"Did you sleep well Tristan?" We asked.
"Yes I fell asleep straight away and have just woken up.
Your big cat was on the bed when I woke up. I forgot to
close the door."
"That's OK with us" said Jasper "I hope it's OK with you
too."
"Yes, no worries. It's not something I would allow in my
house, but I am not in my house."
I don't know why he needs to forbid everything or have
everything forbidden I thought. It was probably something
their experts had said again. I smiled. Oh, no, I thought
suddenly, it's to mark their power. I laughed but it was sad.
I don't know people who do that but I heard it happens
here too, some are a real nightmare to live with. They
should be left alone. That's what I would do and that is
what I was doing. I hoped he wouldn't invite me there until
they opened to the world as I would have to excuse myself,
for sure.

"Are you ready Tristan?" Michael asked.

"Do you want some coffee or some tea?" asked Jasper, "anything to eat?"

Tristan sat down where he sat yesterday and put his notebook and pen on the bed-table that Jasper had brought yesterday.

"Yes, thank you Jasper, I'll have a black coffee with some toast and jam. Is that OK?"

"Sure Tristan. I'll be back in one minute"

"OK Michael, let's start. Yesterday you talked about Habibi, the book and when it came out. Now would you mind telling me what happened? I mean practically. How the world started to change?" asked Tristan.

"Sure" replied Michael.

I turned my chair toward the fireplace, so I was only half way facing them. I stared at the flames. They're always so beautiful and somewhat peaceful. The sound of the wood crackling, I love it. It's so relaxing.

"When the Book came out…you'll read it soon I have a copy for you, I fetched it this morning, I'll give it to you later…it's in my sport bag…well, when the book came out, early in December, nobody really knew what would happen. Everyone was preparing for Christmas and life was its usual self. No one knew how many copies were sold, not even Habibi. He had to wait a month before he would know. Everything went on as usual for a few months."

"Sorry Michael, if I remember well, JR said it started on 21st of December to which you added 2012 and now you are telling us 'all went on as usual for few months'? I don't understand."

"Please Tristan, let me finish," Michael pointed out.

"During those few months, it was winter and a particularly cold winter that year, some villages, communities all around the globe started to live the way Habibi was describing in his book. Everyone carried on, as if nothing happened but they refused to get paid or to pay for anything between one another. The postmen kept working, doctors, the staff in the supermarkets, everyone. Everything seemed to be the same."

"But surely they had to pay taxes; and didn't they have to pay for things that were coming from outside? The shops?" interrupted Tristan.

"And they did," replied Michael, "they created a common account, in which they gave all their wages. The tourists had to pay as usual. They used the money they collected to pay for anything that was needed in the village, to pay the taxes and the gas, electricity, petrol. They decided that from that time forward, at Christmas, people would exchange things they had made and not bought. They were all in control and started via the Internet to create their own protected sites where they could vote between themselves. Some already started the new style bingo. Meanwhile, with spare money and hard work, they also converted all the houses to be self-sufficient and banned plastic and any other polluters. They prepared their fields and land by the side of the streets to be filled with fruit and vegetables for the coming season. They built fireplaces in each house. Everyone started to grow fruit and vegetables at home. With a self-sufficient system, everyone could grow for free, indoors. Of course, they still obeyed the laws of their countries, and the different police forces realized that they could keep their jobs with Habibi's vision. Some became Peacefullers, starting to tattoo their right index finger with a rainbow ring like Habibi had described. Many were on holiday in their villages when it happened and some decided to stay there and not go back to work, joining the local Peacefullers. That was a big problem in the police departments, as well as in many other jobs at that time, the location. People were sent to the other side of their land to do their jobs, which meant they were separated from their loved ones and their homes, even their lands. Therefore they would be less affectionate with strangers and more likely to enforce any laws, wherever they were. If they stayed at home, or in their land, they would have passed on a lot more of what they used to call infractions; infractions that they were known to be continuously committing themselves. It didn't really show, in the police records in those early months. It was just like normal, some policemen changing careers. Habibi had advised everyone not to talk about it at first, not by phone, nor on the net; but only inside each community to start with. The Book started to appear in every pocket. Translations started to appear. It was only in the spring that the first village publicly appeared. It was shown on a video on YouTube on what they had done since The Book came out and the effects it had produced on the inhabitants, the land and the animals. It looked like a paradise was emerging. Of course everyone was following their usual routine, the Christians were going to their churches, and everyone was doing their usual rituals. 'You never know,' people were saying, 'I'd rather keep on believing like before, with all the fears, but I'm happy to change the way our society functions if that will make the world a much better place. That is what all prophets have wanted, isn't it?' Many people hid from others the fact that they now believed in Habibi's spiritual version of Life even though he, himself had asked anyone not to make a religion of his sayings. 'It is just for you to know. But really you don't need to know. You are not even required to believe, but you are required to love one another'."

Tristan was scribbling in his notebook like mad. He was sweating.

Michael kept on:

"Habibi made the people realize that they were ready for this change, that they were responsible for what was happening on Earth, that giving the power to a small group of greedy people had never been proved good for humanity and that life is what humans make of it. Many had started those communities before the Book, but they had always looked like a sect with a long-haired bearded man trying to portray Jesus and forbidding his followers of this, that and the other. Here we only forbid what hurts the planet, plastic is an example, we use hemp biodegradable plastic instead; and what hurts the humans, meat for example, which has been proven to be the cause of many ailments. We don't ban it, but we do ban hunting as it is dangerous for humans but also because using weapons is unequal with the animals. If you want to eat it, kill it with your bare hands! That is how it is now. Most people are therefore vegetarians but you will still find, particularly among the oldest generation, some who are self-destructive and eat meat. They can get their food from some farms. It is getting increasingly rare. What is the point of trying to destroy ourselves? We love Life. It's so free and abundant and beautiful."

"The Vegetarian and Vegan Police are making sure this natural rule is respected" I added.

"Excuse me, what about the non-civilized people JR talked about? What about those who live in tepees?" asked Tristan.

"Tristan, most of the non-civilized people are now civilized. Those who aren't live in the forest but they do obey the law on hunting. That is the only condition for their type of 'freedom'. They have to. The animals now know that we are protecting them. They have a brain and the relationship that we humans have with them has completely changed as you will notice during the time you are here. Those people use our repair centers, some also go to our schools and they even come to the markets; some are very good craftsmen. But none of them hunt."

"So they belong to the Vegetarian Police?" asked Tristan.

"Some of them yes but they all admire the men of the woods who are all vegetarians and most of them are Peacefullers, Vegetarian Police officers and belong to the world army. They are very much respected by everyone, civilized or wild."

"So what about, the Indians? I heard they were allowed to live the way they always did. They were hunters weren't they?" Tristan smiled as if he had found a contradiction. Michael smiled back:

"Tristan, if I specialize in the last 200 hundred years of History, it is because we are not so sure of everything else beforehand. The books were changed, burned, transformed to suit the people in power. How can we believe anything that was taught even when the Ivolution happened? We are still finding a lot of writings that were hidden, everywhere in every corner of the globe, writings that contradicted what was thought before. It is very hard to have a proper understanding of the past. That is why most people prefer to forget that history even existed. The Indians, as you call them Tristan, are spiritual people. When they were given total freedom, they re-installed a lot of their old shamanic ways, using products they were not allowed to use before. They contacted the spirits of their ancestors who asked them to follow that natural order of Life. They are also vegetarians."

Tristan looked up and smiled:

"OK, and what about the Eskimos? Those renowned fishermen?"

"Eskimos were descendants of a family that long ago travelled north as to escape something or someone that was in power in their land. They adjusted, with time, to the very hash conditions of the north. Now that all is free and happy, they have come back down south, to have a better quality life and to leave those barely-inhabitable places, uninhabited."

Tristan was astonished. He was writing and writing again.

"Habibi," Michael went on, "made us notice in his Book that some people who were working for a low wage could hardly afford their rent but they were still giving their time as volunteers, like some richer people were doing, especially the wives of the rich men. The young and some not so young were working freely to gain experience. They all seemed ready to work freely to give and take freely. 'If you love, what you call your modern world', Habibi used to say, 'then you should protect it. You should make sure it will last because at this rate, it will not be long before we will be back in the time of Noah's Arks'. People understood what he meant. Of course, it was simple, money was only there to make people believe that some are more important than others, and that some products are more important than others."

"But surely, isn't it so?" questioned Tristan.

I never heard of such originality before. I know some things are more rare than others, that is why we have local and world galleries and bingos but the idea that someone was more important because of what he does doesn't make sense to me and I know it didn't make sense either to most of us.

"How can a doctor think he is more elevated than a bin man?" asked Michael.

Tristan laughed as if he had heard the most stupid thing ever.

"Well for a start because doctors save lives," replied Tristan "and they study for much more longer than a bin man. Come on, be logical man."

I was very interested to hear what Michael would say.

"Do you think so Tristan?" asked Michael.

"I mean, come on Michael. They had to be pretty humble to accept being lowered to the rest of the people, or probably, they didn't have the choice," added Tristan.

"Really, is that what you think Tristan? Well, let me tell you that without the bin men, or those who clean the streets, there would be much more disease. Disease was often the cause of death in those times. Don't you think they saved lives indirectly including the lives of some doctors, by doing their jobs?"

Tristan was perplexed. I was smiling.

"So what about studies? A doctor needs what, seven, 10 years of study; a cleaner, maybe a week if at all."

"In the old system yes, maybe Tristan but not since the new system has started. As you know through JR, many diseases have vanished due to the change in diet, the use of herbs, the cures that came with the Ivolution. Some cures pre-existed but were hidden for business purpose, others were found very quickly, and the general happy and free lifestyle has brought a stress-free life for everyone. Some people still want plastic surgery, mostly the transsexuals, but that is becoming less and less frequent because, you may have noticed, most people are seen to be perfect as they are. And the new generations are very beautiful, I think. Fewer and fewer are born disabled, due to the good karma everyone maintains, but also many disabilities were due to poor lifestyle or were caused by medical drugs. Habibi told us that during these dark times, many spirits were pretending to be disabled in their incarnation to have a 'less stressed' life, and many were asking God, The Father to be born disabled as well. It was a way to be taken care of. People learn how to take care of themselves at school as well as how to self-treat common ailments. Doctors, nowadays, work mostly in repair centers. They are taught to cut, to stitch, and to care. And more and more robots are performing those jobs also. Some people may want to learn it all but the majority specialize in one-thing and have diverse occupations on the side. What is feeling superior when everyone can have it all? It is feeling loved!" Michael concluded.

I applauded.

"With no money, we have no limitations," Michael added.

"We are creating this new society of abundance, freedom, love and peace for all. With time, it will get better and better. We are all so excited to wake up everyday," Michael added "and we have not yet started to explore space! We're so busy dealing with the earth, and clearing up the old satellites and rubbish rotating around it."

"So what happened from spring that year, 2013 in my calendar that is?" asked Tristan when he finished writing. "Many videos started to show all those little places that had evolved to freedom and happiness to everyone around the globe. They connected with one another and started to exchange supplies and ideas. The governments saw what was happening but they were too busy creating wars in the Middle East and other places, wars to make people believe that governments were needed. But people who were becoming more and more aware of Habibi's writings, no longer believed in them and their propaganda. The first city started to follow Habibi's plan and joined the online community, and then a second, a third, a fourth…it didn't stop. Orders were given by the old governments, who started to join forces around the globe, to stop it happening, but more and more police and military were joining the Peacefullers and weren't following those orders. They were simply doing their job, making sure peace is respected and all people were free. They were so loved by the people that they received even more than everyone else. It seems the governments forgot that the police, the army and other forces are mostly composed of the general public who of course now defended the public before greedy governors and those few who pretended to be kings or sovereigns. The first nation declared itself open, ID free and money free, then a second, then a third… In a year, the world changed itself to what it has become now. We are still consulting Habibi for advice on most matters."

"I'm surprised" said Tristan "I was expecting rebellions,

murders, killings, bombings…"
"Why is that Tristan?" asked Michael.
"Well, I believe most humans are stupid and bad. They need to be controlled and often disciplined."
We both laughed, Michael and I. Jasper had long gone back upstairs and Lou was in the garden.
"Don't forget Tristan, we have the 'Bonding Lights' team who make sure no-one is hiding or carrying weapons" Michael added.

"Anyway, to cut a long story short, it took a year to change the world. Few regents of the time called their followers into underground cities that we discovered a few years later when they opened their gates, gasping for natural light and in the east a nation encircled themselves with a wall. I am sure you know it through JR."
"Yes, he already told me. He also talked about a queen who is thought to have escaped to space," replied Tristan.
Michael looked at me and smiled.
"Oh, Tristan. JR is a fan of parapsychology, the aliens and stuff. Of course he thinks this conspiracy to be true. He is so gullible." He laughed. I smiled.
"Well, we will never know" I answered.
"I hope they have para-asteroids and that their spaceship is not rusting away," Michael added. "When most of the world changed, we organized a big online event to find out which town or village had changed first. They had to prove by any means the date, the place and the actions. The winner and therefore the one who made us decide to use the 21st of December as the new starting date, was a small village in Ireland. The inhabitants filmed themselves in front of their town that they had renamed 'Aquarius' on the 21st of December of that year and changed most of the names of their villages streets, naming them after the names of their people, or pages on the internet that were inspirational and awakened, as well as modern authors and

artists, and local heroes; but keeping the names of those that had brought something beautiful to humanity."

Jasper came down the stairs and went into the kitchen. Then he came back to us.

"Hello boys, I am off to rehearsal with the band. I will see you later. Michael, there's a lot of stuff in the freezer, so help yourself and see what the boys want, OK? Enjoy the movie, all of you, I've seen it many times but I prefer everything that is Post-History, so don't mind me. Bye bye."

"Have a great evening Jasper," I said.

Michael got up and went to talk privately with Jasper, Tristan was focused on his notebook, writing and underlining stuff he had previously written.

When Michael came back, Tristan was ready to keep going:

"Thank you Michael, I'm sure there is much more that you could say on how everything happened in that first year."

"Of course, there is," replied Michael, "in fact, there are many films that have been made and books too. You can get a few Post-History books and documentaries, if you like. There's a lot of information on the net," Michael added.

"OK, thanks but I'd like to know what happened to Habibi meanwhile. I know I'm going to see the movie but as you didn't tell me if it stops at the Book, The Ivolution or later, I'm wondering what happens to him after the book came out. You said that in the late spring that followed, he was exposed to the world and the authorities tried to ridicule him?"

"Yes, I did say that yesterday. A few months after his book came out, as life was still going the same way, apparently, Habibi, with the sale of his book, could finally afford a place for himself. He moved to the Pyrenees where he still lives now. You will find his house has evolved since he bought it. It was a very small stone house, half demolished, at the end of a footpath, surrounded with forests and fields with streams of fresh water. That was all he could afford. Now, as you will see on Sunday, when you'll meet him, it is Sunday isn't it?" asked Michael.

"Yes, it's Sunday" I replied.

"Well, you will see it has been built up. Habibi is still living in the same house, which is now a little larger, and many of his friends and family have built homes along the footpath to it or not too far away. He didn't think his book would affect the world, he just wrote what was in him, you see, Tristan. He didn't expect anything. He thought he would have to keep paying all his life, that life would carry on in exactly the same way. He never even expected that the Book would cover the cost of the humble house he'd always liked, so he had planned to keep working, behind a sewing machine for the rest of his life, as he had done before the Book."

"You mean he never tried to become famous? Even when he saw sales were very good?"

"Habibi didn't do that. No, he wanted to be happy, at peace and free like I told you. Of course he became famous, even more with the transformations of the world that he started. Let me tell you Tristan, you are very lucky. Many people would love to be in your place on Sunday. It is the only day when Habibi doesn't receive. Every other day, thousands of pilgrims go to see him. Some say he became the greatest healer of all time but I believe, it is faith that heals and not the person," Michael added.

"Yes, Tristan, it is true what Michael is telling you. Indeed, we are very lucky. He might even speak to you," I confirmed.

"What do you mean, he 'might even speak to me'? Of course he'll speak to me, I am going there to ask him questions. He's not like a saint that you can't touch, is he?" replied Tristan nervously.

Neither Michael, nor I replied.

CHAPTER XIV

It sometimes felt like Tristan could not grasp the beauty of it all.

Michael got up and went to get the dinner ready.
"Do you need any help?" I asked him.
"I'm good JR; I'll give you a shout. Maybe, you would like to set up the table? Unless you prefer to eat on the sofa?" Tristan asked for the table, so I helped. We left him to his notes.

"He seems a bit lost, Tristan, doesn't he?" Michael asked.
"Well, I'm not sure what to think. When we went to the market, he seemed to be happy and enjoying it but when we told him about the Trans- and Dope-Olympics he freaked out. Since then he has been very reserved and focused on his mission," I replied.
"Well. I guess he is doing his job as best he can. I remember how difficult it was when the uncivilized world opened. Even if Tristan said that they had recently evolved in his Island with a revolution, I think they are as civilized

as the anarchists who were behind the wall: they haven't really evolved for 100 years. Do you want to know the old name of Tristan's Island, the name he probably still calls it?" asked Michael.

"No, thank you Michael, I don't have any use for this information."

After dinner, we came back to the living room and I took my favorite seat near the fireplace.

"Michael, yesterday, you referred to Habibi saying that, I quote: 'The atheists liked him but wanted him to remove any connections or any writings on the source and the creation of the world, its history he had spoken about.' What did he say?"

"You will read it in the Book" I replied.

"Indeed Tristan, you will read it in the Book. But if you want, I can summarize it before we watch the movie."

"That would be great" he replied.

"In his Book, he explains, at some point, that we are all spirits incarnated in bodies. It started very long ago in a place, which has no real name. It is just there, eternal. All the spirits live in this place."

"Heaven?" Tristan quickly interrupted.

"Yes, something like that. Although Habibi didn't use this name, but called it Home. He said that one day during a meditation he saw a Christian god who asked him for obedience. Habibi asked him, 'And who created you?' The god screamed 'No!' and disappeared. Soon after he found himself in front of a god with an elephant's head who asked him for obedience. Habibi again asked 'Who created you?' And again, this god said 'No!' and disappeared. It went on and on until finally there were no deities in front of him but everything was white around him, all misty-like. He asked if he was alone in such a place and as he did, the mist seemed to disappear. Two pure silhouettes appeared on either side of the central aisle of what looked like the inside of a pure white temple. They were hiding their faces with their hands, not wanting to look at him. Habibi became obstructed from going on and silenced from the need to speak. Then, slowly, he came back to reality. Another time, it was during the night, in a pure moment of illumination around 3am in the morning. That was when Habibi started to have problems sleeping. Words were coming into his mind, sentences were banging inside his head until he articulated them. Until he made those sentences publicly available on the Internet, he was prevented from sleeping. Everyone was asking him to write a book but he refused. He saw the creation of the world. Many spirits asked The Source of All, Habibi calls it Dad, to create a place for all spirits to be incarnated, for all spirits to be free, for all spirits to be in control, a place of pleasure and abundance for all, a second home but without Dad there for a change. They asked if He really loved them, unconditionally, why were they stuck in a spirit world? Why, when they could enjoy much more? Dad was not impressed by their asking, he knew what was going to happen and how many spirits would suffer. His First was pleading for those spirits to get what they wanted and Dad told him to do what he wanted to do but that he will have to care about it and that he himself will suffer, know misery, torture and many horrible things that don't need to happen. Anyway loving the spirits so much, he wanted to give them what they wanted. With a breath, The First created the known universe, a bubble floating in Home, a very precious bubble indeed, where they created earth and all that it is needed to maintain Life for the many incarnations of the spirits. All was inside it, animals, mountains, seas, cities, and villages. Everything was there, pretty much as it is today but of course in complete respect for the planet and for each other. Everything was perfect, with everything and everyone being true to themselves, completing each other in the maintenance of this beautiful garden. One spirit, loved by Dad as much as all the other spirits, was frustrated at not being the First of the Source. All the others also knew they were not the First but accepted why there is only one First, and that nobody else can be him, the one many call the one and only Son of God. At first all spirits remembered why they were there, and why everyone was eternal. They knew everything, all the plants, all the animals, every incarnated spirit knew everything, but the frustrated ones started to create trouble. Troubles that Dad had foreseen that he knew would happen. At that time, The First was incarnated: he lived on a mountain."

"Like Habibi" I said.

Michael looked at me quickly.

"He was living on a mountain. I cannot tell you which one as the world was such a different world back then. He was not in control, he was making sure that all was running smoothly for everyone, he was caring, as his Dad had asked him. One day the frustrated spirit found him and killed him, 1000 years after the first incarnations. They knew back then that death existed, but the body just disappeared. This was for the spirits who were not happy there and wanted to go back Home. It was the first murder the world and times had witnessed. At that time, the world had a form of Internet, something like we have today in Post-History where everyone is active but instead of using keyboards and screens, they used crystals and telepathy. The frustrated spirit installed himself in place of the First, who was now deceased, and started to wear strange masks and robes asking other spirits for obedience, and not leaving his home that he now called The Church. He asked for fortified palaces to be built for his family, friends and his most fervent followers where they could live an unrestricted life. Battles were starting everywhere, but of course many were convinced it was the real First as they did not believe he had been killed, unlike what many theorists were saying back then when they began to see differences of attitude. Anyway to cut a long story short, it took ages for the frustrated one to gain power over the whole world. Meanwhile, The First, back home, decided to make Life a little less comfortable because the humans, the incarnated spirits, were starting to battle, creating armies and committing the worst crimes one can imagine. If they wanted fears, battles, hatred, and death, then he would create dinosaurs in the hope that it would help the spirits to enjoy life, to live together in harmony and to stop fighting one another. He succeeded for a while. Of course the frustrated one was well protected in his mountain, with most thinking he was the First and he started to spread the idea of Dad full of vengeance. Many, of course, followed him, and believing to be immortal in an immortal world, they gave him power. Slowly he turned everyone to his side and proclaimed himself god. They fought the dinosaurs and discovered meat. He asked everyone to start to feed on animals, and to hunt. He loved it, seeing everyone, getting into killing, including killing one another. Those who refused to kill humans were more inclined to kill animals. Many started to leave the cities for the wild and joined the tribes, slowly converting themselves to hunting, meat and battles. Many started to suffer from very strange ailments as if their bodies were unclean. Anyway, to cut the story short, the Source and his First allowed the frustrated one to be glorious as long as the humans wanted it. It looked like they really loved their killing murderous world. Because of this, many spirits didn't want to be incarnated any more and it got to a stage where most spirits were asking if it wouldn't be better to just destroy it all because it had brought chaos and suffering between the incarnated spirits back on Earth and no one knew how it could change."

I got up and went to fetch some water.

Tristan was just sitting comfortably, listening. Michael picked up the relaxing box.

"I guess it's just another theory," said Tristan.

"Yes, indeed Tristan" replied Michael "I'll be finished soon. The idea of destroying creation was not that interesting but it could serve to change the frustrated one and make him realize how much he was loved by Dad and his Son, the First. So they worked out a plan to recycle the Planet, dispersing the lands, the people, and the languages so as history wouldn't repeat itself. They asked him to make three big boats, where he should house all living creatures and seeds. He should also house himself with his favorite people. This was a way to show him how much Dad and the First loved him, even though he had done terrible wrongdoing. He was given a second chance, and what a chance? They were to teach the world with all the knowledge they had remembered. As from now on, all spirits would not be incarnated with the knowledge of where they came from or indeed any knowledge. It would make it even harder if he tried again to gain power over the world. A second 'circle' started, this time, without cities, a wild world, with a limited life span for each human. The main boat arrived in the middle-eastern world, one boat arrived in the big island, you probably call it America Tristan, and the third boat arrived in the eastern world, around what you know as China Tristan. They had kept a record of everything in each boat and had conjured a plan to once again take over the world. They recorded it all and made pacts amongst themselves, knowing that they would have to ensure that each future generation in their family kept the power they had gained if not obtain more. They had protected themselves in not eating meat but now they will die anyway, they started also and set it as standard for everyone. You might remember the times of the Pyramid, don't you Tristan?"

"Yes, I do," replied Tristan.

"I love the pyramids" I said, "in my books, they say that they were initiation schools."

"Rubbish," Michael continued, "they were tombs. As you

can see they didn't like the idea that they were not immortal any more."

"So The First never came back on Earth? Until, erm, Jesus?" asked Tristan.

"Oh, no, Tristan. He came back many times. But each time he was killed once he became noticed and loved. One time he was called Apopi Alexandru, who was actually resurrected and inspired his murderer to start making mummies, thinking they would also be allowed to come back and resurrect their dead bodies. The First came back everywhere not at once of course, but always bringing the same message to the world, always trying to make them realize the perfection of it all and the infinite love of Dad. Habibi said that when he realized that everything was perfect, he could not stop laughing and crying. A pure hysteria, he recalled, always showing the way to freedom and happiness. In some places, he was revered and had a 'normal' life, in others places he was tortured and murdered. Habibi reminded us that Dad and his First had a Master Plan and that this Master Plan was to give a free, abundant and happy world to all the spirits because they had asked for it. Of course it would be easy for The Source to just destroy the frustrated spirit but being Love, he didn't want to do that and he knew that sooner or later, we humans would realize what was happening once again.

This time the frustrated one didn't just want the world but he wanted to defy Dad by taking over the world where he would be in total control of every supply, every animal, every human who is born on this planet. We also learned that the same frustrated spirit wanted to recycle the planet himself this time, by destroying it completely whilst he escaped to space with its favorites, I prefer to call them demons, and come back when earth was restored. He knew that this time he would not be offered a third chance. Many knew what was happening and were killed and tortured.

When we all realized what was happening, and after reading Habibi's Book, we decided that we would not accept any single person in control, but all of us, forever. Dad had known this all along and had remained hopeful. The wicked spirits are usually very lonesome in our human world now. They are not followed. There are just a few of them, mostly from the oldest generation, those who grew up in the time of History. Habibi added that it was all created on the principle of balance: 'Whatever you give, you get back, good for good and bad for bad in this life or the next'."

"The Law," I added. "OK, can we stop now and watch that movie. It's getting late."

Michael got up and went to fetch the movie. He gave a copy to Tristan with some other DVDs and books he knew would help Tristan with his report. He also gave him the Book.

CHAPTER XV

The plane journey down to Toulouse was fast. Tristan was reading his notes and had started the Book. He was very taciturn, so I listened to some music with my headphones and dozed all the way, Lou was asleep near me.

We stayed two nights with Juliet and Christopher. Juliet is a dancer, we met at school in Brighton when we were young, but she had moved south, for the heat, where she met Christopher. We were still good friends. Christopher was away working on a study project for the reforestation of the Sahara. Juliet told us that now, they not only take vast amounts of fresh water to the desert everyday but also people's excrement. It is no longer sent into the waters like they did back at the end of History. My granddad could not understand how it could have been approved and he told me that Habibi said it came from a wicked plan from the frustrated one. Now, we return our excrement back to the land, as it is meant to be, acting as natural fertilizer. We do the same with ashes. The idea started when we noticed the progress we had made in reforesting areas around the globe that were once damaged, it seems it reconstituted a proper soil much more quickly. We do it bit by bit. It is hard work I've heard. Maybe I'll try and give some time to it, now that

105

I've finished all my usual occupations.

On the first evening, Tristan decided to stay in his
bedroom, reading. He just hand-picked food on his way and
he asked to be left alone.
Of course we didn't mind as we had so much to talk about
since we last met. We went for a walk in the city centre. It is
such a beautiful city with all the food growing everywhere,
the houses either painted or showing the beautiful
brickwork. It is so colorful. And it was much warmer than
at home, at this time of the year. It was very peaceful and
alive. Toulouse is well renowned for it's food, but it is
principally a party and distribution city. Like all cities, and
towns, one can find everything that one needs throughout
the day and the night. Of course, we can't yet say the same
about the Christmas holidays, even though many people are
now beginning to open their restaurants, bars and
nightclubs at this time of the year, especially in the cities.
It's not really like it used to be when we were young.
Anyway, we decided to stop at a restaurant and have dinner.
It is crazy all the dishes they offered on the menu. I think
there was a little competition between the different
restaurants going on: we were asked to judge the meals
afterwards on paper. I enjoyed it; the food had so many
flavors, with their Mediterranean seasoning. I always go for
local dishes. I think it's best. Some people I know,
anywhere they go, choose to eat dishes like those they have
at home, but although we can find almost everything
everywhere around the globe, apart from Tristan's Island
products of course, I prefer to taste the local dishes. I'm not
so passionate about world cuisine when I'm back home,
sometimes a couscous, fajitas, burgers or pizza: food I've
discovered when traveling and continued to enjoy back at
home, but that is all really. The rest of the time, I enjoy my
local recipes, my Sunday veggie roast and my vegan Full
Brits breakfast. I often miss them when I'm away, but at

least I try new combinations.

"Hey look, it's Juliet!" we heard suddenly.
"Hello Luca," said Juliet, "how are you?"
"I'm great, Juliet, my book is still asked for and I am off to Las Vegas next week to give a workshop, so all is going well," replied Luca "what about you Juliet?"
"Oh, I've just come back from performing in Munich."
"Really? Munich? But it's The Dance City of the world? Fabulous! Did you love it?"
"It was brilliant. Yes, and I saw some of my old dance teachers from Dalian, also a great dance city."
"Cool, did I tell you I've been invited to practice in Sydney?"
"No, I didn't know."
"Well, now you do! Do you know what else?"
"No," replied Juliet.
"Well, as I'm getting older, I'm becoming even more of a cleaning maniac, so much so, that I've enrolled to work at the repair centers as a cleaner every morning, wherever I may be. I mean I know we all clean our homes and in front of them, whether we are in private houses or in communal buildings, but I never thought I would clean somewhere else and there are plenty of others like me. I have met lots of new friends, and clients. I guess one can't escape what he or she loves. Saying that, we use more and more robots for many of the jobs and in the years to come, I won't be needed, well only to coordinate the robots. Anyway I am off sweetie pie, see you around."
"That's so good. OK, bye bye then" Juliet replied.

It was like if I wasn't there, with Juliet.
"Who is he?" I asked her.
"Oh, don't mind him. He's a tantric teacher and he wrote a book on The Art of Love. This is the title by the way. He believes that everyone should learn this art that has been so

much condemned throughout History for no other reason than frustration and power. He explained to me once that most people are being taught again on how to make love. Back in History, they used to do it like animals, and many still believe that this is the only way and the only use for it. I think his readers love him. I don't know, I am not into this" she replied, "even if I think I would love it if Christopher could learn and practice it on me without me knowing how to do it. I just want to feel it at its best."

"You haven't changed," I smiled. "Well I guess everyone is different. Anyway he should be more courteous, this kind of career may not last long and he might not get so much love then."

"Yeah, whatever," finished Juliet, "don't forget he also cleans at the repair centers. He might have more of a conscience than you think. Anyway, talking about cleaning, have you heard that there are still some places where women are considered lower than man?" asked Juliet.

"Honestly, I don't mind if a woman wants to take care of her man or woman, but they just don't have that choice. I'd love to find a man to do it all for me. I know some exist, but they are usually gay."

"Well, I don't really know, Juliet. They might be happy as such. Is it really low to do the cleaning, cooking and ironing for the one you love? I don't think so. Everybody does what he or she is meant to do, like the animals, like the plants and minerals, like the sun, like Dad. Personally, I like to do my own cooking and cleaning but if I meet someone then I think we will share the jobs, unless she insists that she prefers this or that. I have no preferences in that matter."

Juliet looked like if she was thinking, then she said:

"Oh, I haven't told you that I'm now a coordinator. You know how I like to organize things and make sure everything runs smoothly. I give some hours at the local city hall and when I am away, I visit and help at their halls.

A lot of work happens online as well. It's easy with our open videoconferences. I love it. It might become my main job when my dancing career stops, although I will surely be teaching it."

"Oh, fabulous!" I exclaimed. I've always been passionate about coordinators and I know one day I will join them: "I would love to do this as well, but for there aren't enough hours in the day and I can only coordinate my days!" I joked.

CHAPTER XVI

On Saturday morning, we took the train to Mazamet, to visit the house where Habibi spent his teenage years. It's now an open museum.

We walked through the town, and stopped for lunch at one of the town's sandwich places. There are a lot of boutiques with products inspired by Habibi for the tourists to take back home. I got three cards, with a picture of Habibi in his teenage years in front of the house, one to send to the animal centre back home, one for Tristan to use as bookmark in the Book and one for me, for my Book.

We waited for at least 30 minutes before we got to the front door; there were so many people. I was amazed mostly by the workshop at the back that belonged to Habibi's dad. It was like being in a history documentary: an incredible place, smelling of wood, where Habibi's dad, granddad and great granddad had spent their life. They had their pictures in there and the guide said that the spiders on the ceiling were the descendants of the ones who were there when Habibi lived there and helped his dad.

Although, we could go to the village near Habibi's house in the mountains where he grew up as a child, we were not allowed to approach the house: it still belongs to his family who often stay there, and one of his nephews actually lives there permanently with his wife. Of course you can get pictures and information on the house in all the boutiques. It was a farm that Habibi's dad had completely remade with wood mostly and stone walls.

Tristan was not talking very much, he was opening all his books one by one, looking everywhere through all the details and so on. He had found his new teachers.

We took an early train back to Toulouse to have a good night's sleep before driving to Lourdes. Juliet had gone out to meet some friends.

Wherever I am, every day of the year, I do the same routine when I wake up, and when I go to bed after my evening acknowledgment. I did Hatsu Rei and drank my blessed glass of water and I prayed:

"Our father who art in heaven, your being is sanctified, your reign is eternally established. Your will is done on earth, in the universe like in heavens. Give us, each day, what we deserve and do not let us submit to anyone else but you by the sacred heart of your unique son. Amen."

CHAPTER XVII

Today was my last full day with Tristan. Tomorrow, I will
be back home before I start travelling again. I had decided
to take at least a year off from everything. We never know
what may happen and before I feel too old I want to do
some last things, like the Muktor winter festival.
I remembered Tristan said that he would love to try those
flying cars, so I made a reservation to pick up one.
I think he was amazed. I drove. It was a shame I could not
let him try to drive one, but he doesn't have a flying car
license and the Peacefullers are everywhere. I didn't want to
take the risk.
"I have decided to let my hair and beard grow," said Tristan
on our way there, "starting today. Also, if you don't mind, I
will not come back to London with you because I want to
go south and have a look at this Sahara project and see what
happens from there."
"Sure Tristan. It was a pleasure to meet you and I hope I
have been able to answer most of your questions, with the
help of Michael of course."
"Oh, Michael is a great teacher. I have many more
questions that I will ask along the way. I am supposed to let

the agency know of my whereabouts, so I will give them a call tomorrow and keep them informed as required. Don't worry, I will give a good report about you and don't forget to write something in the report, JR, if you want. You said you wanted to read it?"

"Oh, I may have a look through it but you wrote a lot and I am not sure I want to hear the history again" I replied "but yes I will write something."

We left the flying car at the rental company and walked to the start of the walk up to Habibi's house. It starts at the Habibi temple, a massive monument with water coming from a grotto.

We stopped on the way to pick up a warm jacket for each of us as it was cold in the Pyrenees. We opted for two long brown coats made of local wool, the same ones the shepherds wear. I knew I would keep and wear this one for years.

We were very lucky as on other days, we would have had to wait ages to get our water bottles filled: it is a custom to bring an empty bottle and fill it with the water from the grotto. Many even bathe in those waters.

Tristan was very excited. He was making some strange signs and gestures in front of the grotto, it was probably some religious ritual he had learned. I didn't know what it meant. "I heard about Lourdes back in the Island, with my parents being Catholics but since the Island closed, we have our own Lourdes. Ours is at the water from the spring where the regent we had at the turn of the millennium was baptized. It is said the water became white like milk when it touched his body. Everyone has to go at least three times in his or her life and touch the water. We also kiss the stone the baby boy lay on. Now, after the revolution, I think people can choose, but some still believe it has curative properties."

"Or herpes!" I added. "Sorry, I'm only joking, although no

one knows really, most people believe it is Habibi who had healed the sick, disabled and blind. They just needed to touch him, people said; although many believe it happens by just looking at him. We don't have many people who are born this way nowadays, people have good karma these days and some spirits don't want to be born needy anymore. My granddad used to say, and Michael confirmed, that in his time, some people were trying everything possible not to be slaves, even pretending to be or making themselves disabled. It was so sad. He said that Habibi told them that even many spirits chose to be born this way. But there are theories that it may be the water from the grotto that people drank on their way to Habibi's house that healed them."

"Yeah, well, that is what I believe. This water is miraculous."

"I actually believe it is the faith that heals. Tristan, do you want to go in Habibi's Temple first? Or shall we go up now?"

There were large speakers in the area with a low ambient style of music incorporating various religious and pagan songs: monastic, tribal, angelic songs, slowly released one by one on this continuous melody. Habibi himself makes some of those mixes but he is more renowned for his Christmas mixes that he gives to the world, one each year. Every 15 minutes, the bells where ringing, one toll for 15 minutes past the hour, two on the half hour, and three tolls for 15 minutes before the hour. At each hour, they played Habibi's hymn.

It was extraordinary.

"I think we should wait after our return to do the boutiques…what do you think Tristan?" I asked.

He was touching the walls of the grotto, going on his knees as if he was submitting himself to unseen forces.

Finally he got up and said: "OK, let's go up. I don't want to go in the temple if it is not Catholic anymore."
I called Lou who was sniffing around.

The pathway was small. Plants and trees from all over the world were growing everywhere, there were seats on the side, many of them overlooking amazing views. You could also see pieces of art that people had left in homage to Habibi. The same music that we heard in Lourdes was slowly released through the foliage, at a lower volume so as to mix with the sounds of nature. Many animals were eating from the abundant food all around.
"Tristan, can you see all the animals?" I asked him.
"Yes, I can. It's very strange to see them all together, not scared of us anymore. I don't really understand how it can be. I guess it's because it's a sanctified area and has always been connected to the grotto at the bottom," he replied.
"Tristan, on your travels you will notice that this not only happens here but everywhere. The animals know that we are protecting all of them, they are very grateful that they can find all types of food everywhere and don't have to risk coming into private gardens to feed. It is like it is meant to be: forever joy, peace, abundance and freedom for all."
"Well, it surely looks like the Garden of Eden I had in mind," he concluded.

I waited for Tristan at what seemed like every bench; he walked very slowly and he seemed to find it hard to go up the hill.
When we arrived at Habibi's land, we passed by the main pathway where many of his friends and family had built their houses. It was beautiful, a variety of old-fashioned stone houses, with flowers, plants, trees, fruits and vegetables growing everywhere. Chickens, cats, horses, goats, rabbits and dogs were running free to name just a few; I'm sure I saw a stag. It was a total fairyland, with

flower banderoles and natural decorative handmade crafts everywhere with the same music continuing. Sometimes, it was a real choir, other times a mix, never the same, never ending. The walls were inscribed with poems, and covered with pictures and gifts that people had left on their way to Habibi's house. There were tables for tourists to eat, where men and women in robes usually served the pilgrims. None were open today, however it smelled of grilled chestnuts.

Tristan was looking everywhere, by the windows into the houses. I felt a bit ashamed. I was glad it was Sunday as no pilgrims were around. Only a few of the monks and nuns who usually helped with the services were out, taking care of the vegetation or speaking with the animals. They didn't engage with us; they probably thought we were some of Habibi's relatives visiting him on a quiet day.

Habibi was in front of his house bare chested, cutting some wood. 'Not bad for a 78 year-old man', I thought. When he noticed us, he stopped, put down his axe and smiled at us. He looked about 40, a short trim black beard with a few white hairs and very short black hair. He looked like he does on the Internet; I had always assumed he used old pictures from the time of the Ivolution. He looked very athletic for his age. 'Well, if he had a self-destructive youth as it is described in the movie, he repaired himself well, now that he is happy' I thought again. I knew his face but I had never seen his body before and I was very surprised.
Tristan was staring at him. He was paralyzed.
Lou ran towards him.

"Good day," Habibi finally said with a big smile, stoking Lou.
Tristan was behaving strangely, now approaching Habibi slowly, looking only at his own feet and he stopped a few meters before Habibi and remained with his head down.
I walked towards Tristan and went to shake Habibi's hand.

'He is strong' I kept thinking, 'much stronger than I.'
Tristan didn't move, as if he was waiting to be invited.
"You must be Tristan" Habibi said out loud, with a straight voice.
I could see Tristan was trembling and beads of sweat started to run down his cheeks.
"It is an honor to meet you," said Tristan. "Indeed, I am Tristan and as you know I come from the Island which closed its frontiers to the world before the turn of the millennium. I am here today to ask you if you would not mind writing a word on the report I am bringing back home. It would help, I think."
Tristan moved a few steps forward and held out a pen and piece of paper for Habibi to write on. Habibi took them and went to a table that was not too far away, sat down and wrote something. I couldn't see what he was writing.
Tristan looked at me and said in a very low voice:
"As soon as he gives me the paper back, I am saying goodbye. I am going back to Lourdes. It is too much for me here. I don't feel right. I will be waiting for you near the grotto."

Habibi, as if he heard, came straight back to us and gave the paper to Tristan.
"Nice to have met you" he said.
Tristan excused himself and left, as if in a hurry, and without looking back at us. He didn't even look at what Habibi just wrote.
"You see" said Habibi, "he reminds me so much of the History people. Anyway young man, I can see you are a bit skinny like I was at your age. Are you doing any exercise?" he asked me.
I was surprised, I never expected him to talk to me more than 'hello' or 'good day' or 'nice to meet you' but he was speaking to me.
"Yes, I do the Salutation to the Sun, every morning when I

take my dog out after the first part of my morning routine," I replied.

"I am going to tell you my secret. Every morning, I do 100 press-ups, 100 abs and 100 squats before I log on to be in contact with the world. If you find it difficult at first, you may want to do one of each to start with and everyday you add one more until you can do 100...in 100 days' time. When I started to repair myself, I used to do it in morning, before lunch and in evening but now I only do it once a day. You can always add those weight jackets or straps we have nowadays. They are great. I use a 50-kilo one. I just want to keep fit, I don't need to build muscle anymore." I looked at him surprised and I thanked him.

"Now" he added "I am going to give you another secret. There is another way down to Lourdes from here that very few people know about and it leaves from behind my house. I call it the 'bells tunnel'. You might like to pass by there. Don't take the pathway on the left you will encounter on your way down, unless you want to go straight to The Spacials. Please keep it to yourself, both are secret." I felt so honored, me who thought I would find the guy on a throne, untouchable. I had it all wrong, maybe because it was Sunday. I was very grateful to the agency to have arranged this meeting.

"I hope you enjoy the Spacials tonight. I won't be coming. Tomorrow, it is Monday and besides receiving all the pilgrims and taking care of my house, the plants, the animals and my loved ones, I want to finish the new chimney I am building in my bedroom before the return of the harsh weather we get around here. So I must hurry. I love fireplaces, and I am so pleased to know this winter I will fall asleep hearing the wood burning alongside the purring of the cats sleeping on my bed, and around my bedroom. I have a chimney in most of my rooms, bathroom, living room and kitchen. Do you have a fireplace?"

"Oh, yes, I have one in my lounge and one in my kitchen."
"At cooker height, in the kitchen?" he asked.
"Yes, I think it is best. I use it a lot, and to keep the kettle warm, like you said in your Book," I replied. "I think all the houses now have fireplaces Habibi, even in London and New York."
"Oh, that's great. I wasn't sure. Some people seem to be so against it. Anyway, you should try this recipe from where I grew up, potato chips and wild mushrooms fried on the fire. Cook them separately, and add parsley with some garlic. I love it with some lettuce leaf seasoned with hemp oil and lemon juice. Have a blessed life JR, enjoy," he finally concluded.

"Thank you Habibi" I replied. I was holding a tear. I wanted to hug him. I felt so much love vibrating around me. It was incredible. I smiled. I didn't want to leave. Habibi was standing in front of me, he suddenly, hugged me and said "you always have the choice to come here, and help like the monks and nuns you have seen on your way here. They come and go, only a few seem truly dedicated to the place. It's fine by me; they are free like everyone else. They tend to see this place as a retreat and it is often full. I am sure I'll meet you again sometime, and hopefully a bit more muscled."

He let go.
I can't say how I felt. I wanted to shout, "I love you. I want to stay." This love energy was unbelievable; I can't begin to describe it with words. I suddenly felt like I was washed of everything, like my body was only a fine membrane and inside only light. The light suddenly exploded, white light was pouring out of me from everywhere. That is how it felt. It took me a few minutes to regain control.
"Here, this is for you" Habibi was holding a little fabric bag.
"For me?" I asked as if I was not alone. I think I blushed.

"Nothing much, my local production to help you tonight to enjoy the dance and a little mounted carved stone that I have blessed. You can wear it if you want. Now I need to get going with this wood before it gets too dark. It's getting darker much earlier at this time of the year. It was a pleasure to meet you."

"Oh, no. It was a real pleasure to meet you. I am sorry I didn't bring anything to give you," I said, feeling very ashamed.

"I have all that I need and more young man. If you want to give me something, then do your best with Tristan in order for him to encourage his Island to be free. That would be the best present we could receive nowadays for them and for us."

"Well, I'm sorry but from tonight or tomorrow morning, I won't be of any further help. My assignment terminated here today. I can only tell you I gave my best."

"Then you just gave me your present. Thank you JR. It makes me very happy indeed. Well done. Now let's wait and see," he finished.

CHAPTER XVIII

Tristan was indeed waiting near the grotto. He was reading. "You've been a long time," he remarked.

"Yes, I'm sorry Tristan. It took me ages to leave. I loved it up there, didn't you?"

"Oh! Yes. It was very inspirational, I can say, but a bit too much for me like I told you when we were there. That man is something for sure but I still believe the Christ will come from the sky!"

"Like Habibi" I replied.

"Pardon? Did you say like Habibi?" Tristan asked surprised.

"Well, yes. Isn't it written in some books? Like Habibi said, 'we don't need to wait for the guy to make this world as it should be. When he comes, the world will be ready. Hopefully it will be from the sky, that would be so sensational, a bit like superman…people need to see sensational power to believe in something it seems'. Not to add that many have tried with subliminal images, often projected on clouds, to imitate the second coming. It often looked totally amazing but so unreal" I laughed.

Tristan whitened.

I encouraged him to get up and we went toward the boutiques; many were still open. I made Tristan notice that nowadays, machines and robots performed many activities to alleviate the human labor.

"Everything is perfect," I told him, "we have been made perfect. And as long as everyone does what he or she loves then he or she completes everyone else and brings his or her contribution to the world. Of course, many are trying to imitate others, mostly the youth really, but they always end up doing what he or she loves. That's life. Everyone wants it to work."

We sat in a 'tea and pot' drinking place and I ordered a chamomile tea with honey and lemon. Tristan ordered a black coffee. I also asked for the grass menu list.

"Can I have a look at the report now Tristan?" I asked. He had written almost everything that Michael and I had said. He didn't talk about Habibi's version of Pre-History and History as I guess, anyone, back in his Island, will be able to read it straight from Habibi's Book. I was very interested to see what Habibi had written and I looked for his page by the end of the notebook. He had written in capital letters:

'YOU ARE ALLOWED TO BE FREE! YOU ARE ALLOWED TO BE HAPPY! YOU ARE ALLOWED TO BE PEACEFUL! YOU ARE ALLOWED TO BE RESPECTFUL! ENJOY' and he had signed it with his usual signature. It's like a cross with a circle underneath and a stroke up.

Tristan pointed to the next page and said:

"Here, you can write something JR."

"OK," I said. "Can I borrow your pen?"

I decided to keep it short and encouraging, I wrote, also, in capital letters:

'(-: JUST BE :-)' written of course with a little smiley before and after, as I like to do, followed by my signature JR.

CHAPTER XIX

"Do you want to come to the Spacials tonight Tristan?" I asked.

"I don't know what is it?" he replied.

"Oh, of course" I said. "They are a group of musicians and artists, many people also call them 'The Techno Angels' as that used to be their name. They have various branches but the core is based not too far from here. They play every night to the public. It is said that Habibi dances to the sound of the Spacials that he can clearly hear from the back of his house, when the wind blows from the west. If we'd have been here last Saturday for Habibi's birthday, we wouldn't have been able to move at all. I'm thinking of coming for his 80th birthday as he usually makes a disc jockey surprise appearance at the Spacials' decks, especially for big birthdays. I have a copy of the last two on my music player if you want to listen to them."

"I think I'll pass on that one. I might well go tonight. I'm not sure yet. Tomorrow I am going south like I said this morning. I'm not sure I want a late night," replied Tristan.

"It's up to you. You can always go there early and be back

for midnight. You need to get fit from what I can see and dance is the most fun," I added.

Even if Tristan was my age, he looked much older. Honestly, I would have described him as 54 or 55 year old man. When I saw him going so slowly up the hill to Habibi I thought it would be nice to give him one small last kick, and it seemed the perfect time. I mean I know I am thin but I am looking young and I am fit and I am going to try to build some muscle with the technique Habibi talked about. We will see.

Tristan, at the end, came to the party. He didn't dance, nor drink any beer. He had some grass. I think he was now relaxed and ready to carry on his work. 'I gave him a good introduction' I thought 'what else can I teach him?' I will surely give him my email address in case he wants to contact me but I doubt he will want to open a world email address because he won't be able to connect through his Island account.

I was dancing when I recognized Maria dancing not too far away.
I went over to her.
"Hey Maria, what are you doing here?" I asked her, almost shouting. The music was so loud.
"JR, no way! You're here! What a surprise!" she screamed running up to me and hanging onto me for a few long seconds.
"Hey what is this you have around your neck? I love it!" Maria was staring at the little stone that I had talked to. I started to feel the stone palpitating again and hear her saying "Yes."
"Do you want it Maria? I found it and it told me its story. I'll tell you in a minute. I think it loves you already."
I took it away from my neck and gave it to her.
"Oh, do you mind if I don't take the lace, I like the one I

already have and can use that."

She held the amethyst pendant all the time that I told her what had happened between the stone and I, and then she fixed it around her neck.

I was happy. Now I had this empty lace to which I could attach Habibi's gift. "It is all so perfect!" I shouted. Maria looked at me and we started to shout "It is all so perfect!" People around us started to say the same. I think that Javier, the Spacials' disc jockey at the deck, heard because straight away he played his own 'It is all so perfect' techno tune. On the dance floor it was madness.

CHAPTER XX

I had a great night at the party. It was so much fun with Maria. She introduced me to her new man, a good and funny man. We laughed so much. It was giant!

I joined Tristan for breakfast. I only slept 3 hours and thought I would go back to bed as soon as we had separated.

He was showered and freshly dressed, in his usual old History school-type look, and his bags were with him. I noticed that he had done many boutiques yesterday after we'd had tea. He even had one of those white robes the monks and nuns always wear on Habibi's birthday and other occasions.

"Well I think it's time to say goodbye," Tristan told me, five minutes after I sat down, "but before we do, I would like you to give me the recipe of that jam we ate on Monday, the dandelion jam. I loved it but with everything going on, I completely forgot to ask you."

"Oh, I'm glad you loved it. It's true you did not make any comments. Well it is very simple. All you need is 365 dandelion flowers, I tend to pick mine in the middle of nature, far from the roads, even though we no longer have any pollution. I think the flowers are happier and therefore give a better taste. Then you need to take all the yellow petals out, and bin the green bits. In my family, we like to let the petals dry in the sun before we put them in a jam cooking pot, but it is not necessary. You can use them fresh. Anyway, you add one-and-a-half liters of water, two sliced oranges, skin-on, and two sliced lemons again with their skin. When it boils, let it simmer for one hour on a low heat, and then filter it by pressing the mixture through muslin. Add one kilo of sugar and cook for around 45 minutes, or until it solidifies when cooled. Pour it into jars, seal them and turn them upside down until cold: the jelly will last longer this way."

Tristan was copying the recipe into a separate notebook, a much smaller one he took from his the inside pocket of his jacket.

"Thank you JR. I really appreciate it. In half an hour, I am taking a train to Tarbes, then onto Perpignan where I will fly south to Marrakesh."

"I hope you have reserved your seats," I said.

He looked at me surprised.

"Why? It's free everywhere, no?" he asked.

"Sure but that doesn't mean that it's not full. What do you think? We need to book for trips, for the cinema, to reserve a car…I did tell you about that and we've been very lucky so far to be able to take the first train and plane without prior booking. If something is booked, you look for the next one that's available. There are plenty of companies offering different levels of comfort, food, drinks, pot and services for different tastes. Some don't offer anything but the travel and of course, they are usually less full. You

should get online. Have you been online yet?" I asked.
Tristan was looking confused.
"No, not yet. It's already so much, I'm not sure I'm ready to
see what the online world web has become."
"I guess there's a bit of everything for everyone. But if
anything is illegal in life, such as hunting, then it is illegal on
the web, such as hunting games. There is a lot of
information that is worth looking at as well and of course
all the bingos and stuff."

"OK, I might go on a computer and book my trip. Do you
mean I might not be able to leave today?"
"No, I am sure you'll find a way. There are a lot of routes
you can take; there are always many options available.
Anyway, if you need to contact me, here is my card."
I gave him one of my little cards with my cyber contact
details including email address and the link to my
loveoneandother.com social networking page, "I'm staying
here until early afternoon and then I am going back to
Brighton. I've decided to register Just Real as my real name
since you were so confused with JR, at least these initials
will now stand for something. I'm going to nap this
morning but don't hesitate if you need anything. You know
where to find me."
"Is it possible for me to go to the train station and book
from there?"
"Sure Tristan" I replied.

"Well, I'll do that then. I'm thinking taking the first train
available out of here."
"You might not like to take the Goth or freak show train" I
laughed.
Tristan looked straight into my eyes, waited few seconds
and said
"Thank You."
"Keep in touch please" I asked before we said farewell to

each other.

CHAPTER XXI

I took the evening train from Gatwick to Brighton.
When we stopped at Haywards Heath, I was half awake,
thinking of all that had happened, all that Michael had said
about History. I could not understand how all this
happened and I were very happy I had made the choice not
to study it. It seemed like everything we know is theory.
Nothing is assured. There were so many lies, books burned
and ideas destroyed. How can anyone pretend to know the
exact truth about history? There were too many wicked
people in power all along, everywhere, to be able to trust
what they have left behind. When I think there were times
when people didn't know how to read? It still sounds
unbelievable and I think it is only a legend. 'I mean,
imagine, if the population didn't read? The people in power
who could read and write would use their superiority,
wouldn't they? To blind the people for as long as they

could! They could re-write anything they liked and burn or bury the originals' I thought.

I opened my eyes and in front of me she was seated. She was there again, the same girl from last Saturday.
"You are not going to escape this time," she said.
"What are you talking about?" I replied, blushing.
"Hello mister JR" she smiled at me "I have been looking for you. I am Eve."
I didn't know what to make of it.

She added: "I want to know everything that has happened to you since I saw you last week. I've been thinking about you non-stop and I have travelled all the streets of Brighton looking for you, taking the trains in the evening just looking for you. And now that you are here, I won't let you go. Never ever!"
So I smiled and I started:
"The day I saw you, I woke up listening to my favorite track 'You have this world on your doorstep'. I waited until the end of the song, went to the kitchen and poured myself a glass of water. When I returned to my bedroom, I lit The Candle, and consecrated it to Habibi's special day.
"I am alive," I said out loud as if words were coming from all my being, "Thank You."

'In memory of all the spirits who have
suffered in this earth's incarnation and all the
spirits who have been so sad back Home.

And DAD.'